"I expect you'll be moving on?"

Holly didn't try to hide the rudeness in her voice.

Nick's lids came down swiftly over his eyes, his face expressionless. He said, "I've made no definite plans. I may stick around here for a while."

"I see."

His brows rose. "My being here doesn't bother you, does it?"

Holly laughed. "Why should it? You're nothing to me now."

His blue eyes were suddenly cold as ice as they came up to meet hers. "Was I ever?"

For a long moment Holly could only stare wordlessly at the man who had walked out and never even bothered to call; the man who had meant everything to her. Unable to stand it any longer, she got abruptly to her feet. "I'm very tired," she said. "Good night."

SALLY
WENTWORTH

say hello to yesterday

Harlequin Books

TORONTO • LONDON • LOS ANGELES • AMSTERDAM
SYDNEY • HAMBURG • PARIS • STOCKHOLM • ATHENS • TOKYO

Harlequin Presents edition published April 1981
ISBN 0-373-10426-X

Original hardcover edition published in 1981
by Mills & Boon Limited

CHAPTER ONE

THE TWICE-WEEKLY FERRYBOAT, which was the only means of reaching the Greek island of Kinos, chugged its way noisily across the still blueness of the Mediterranean, creating a wake that gradually diminished until only minute ripples were left to lap against the rocks that formed jagged promontories guarding the wide bay and the entrance to the harbor of Melmia. The deck of the boat was crowded with goods—drums of fuel, crates of livestock, sacks of fruit and vegetables—leaving little room over for the passengers, who were mostly native Greeks, from their dark hair and olive complexions. But here and there the lighter coloring of travelers from more northern climates could be seen as they stood together in small groups, guarding their luggage.

One girl, though, her shoulder-length fair hair blown into disarray by the breeze created by the boat's passage, stood alone by the rail, gazing intently at the approaching harbor as if searching for something. But it was well into the afternoon now, the sun still high in the summer sky, and there was little or no movement on the jetty or on the few fishing caïques or holidaymakers' yachts tied up against the wall. Disappointed, Holly Weston drew

back from the rail and went back to her extremely
uncomfortable seat on top of a couple of stacked
crates of beer. Hooking her equipment case off her
shoulder, she placed it carefully on the deck between her sandaled feet, safe from any chance
knocks or kicks, and leaned back against some
balks of timber, relaxing and soaking up the sun.

She supposed it had been too much to hope for
that Felix Riddell's yacht would be in harbor. A few
good photographs of that would at least have been a
start to her assignment. Now she would just have to
wait around until the millionaire recluse made up
his mind whether or not he would finally grant her
the interview that her paper had been trying so desperately hard to obtain for the last two months.

The odor of pine filled Holly's nostrils as the sun
brought the fragrance out of the wood she was leaning against. Around her she could hear the voluble
chatter of the other passengers, pitched high to
cover the noise of the old engines as they chugged
protestingly along. The crew began to shout to one
another as they entered the bay, and one of them
came over to her and said something she didn't understand, motioning her to get off the crates of
beer, which were obviously of far more importance
than the passengers. With a sigh, Holly lifted her
bag again and dragged her suitcase out of the way.

As the boat edged its way slowly to the jetty, one
or two men appeared, and in a desultory way caught
the ropes thrown to them and made them fast
around a couple of metal bollards. The engines
groaned to a stop and the rusty anchor cable
shrieked protestingly down, setting one's teeth on

edge until it hit bottom and stopped at last. The crew exchanged greetings and news with the men on the jetty for several minutes before they unhurriedly decided to put the gangplank in place and let the passengers off. Holly waited with resigned patience, used to the procedure by now; it had been like this all day, ever since they had set off from Piraeus at five in the morning. No one hurried; it was as if they had all the time in the world. Which they probably had, she admitted to herself, but the boat had stopped at so many islands that Holly had lost count, and it had been a long, tiring day in a temperature that seemed at least twenty degrees hotter than in England yesterday morning. She longed to shower and to rest in a cool, shaded room, preferably with a soft, comfortable bed on which she could catch up on her lost sleep.

At last the gangplank was secured and the small crowd of Greeks who had been pressing against the rail surged off, laden with bags and parcels. Holly followed more slowly, the only tourist to get off the boat at this stop. Her case wasn't excessively heavy; dozens of earlier foreign assignments had taught her to travel as lightly as possible, but it was awkward with the heavy shoulder bag, and by the time she reached the end of the jetty she had to stop for a breather. The town of Melmia spread in an untidy jumble of white, square-shaped houses around the edge of the bay like giant cubes of sugar, nearly all of them single-storied with only an occasional brightly-painted shutter or door to break up the harsh whiteness. Behind the houses rose rather barren-looking hills with only a few small groves of olive trees on their slopes. A brown outcrop of rock stretched out toward the sea, where it formed the promontories on either side of the bay.

For a moment Holly hesitated, wondering which way to turn to find a decent hotel. In any other country she would have tried to ask in either French, German or Spanish, all of which she spoke fairly well. But she knew hardly a word of Greek, and shrank from the idea of entering one of the little shops that bordered the harbor and getting involved in lengthy directions. Then she caught sight of a two-storied building a few hundred yards to her left, nearer where the pleasure boats were moored, and picked up her cases to head in that direction. By the time she reached it she could feel the perspiration soaking into her thin T-shirt. At least her instinct had led her right, for the building had a terrace outside set with tables and chairs and shaded by a trellis that supported an ancient vine with dark green leaves and bunches of fat purple grapes. The name "Taverna Helios" was painted above the door in what had once been bright red lettering, which had faded to a soft rose in the sun.

There were several men sitting at tables at the back of the terrace where the shade was deeper, and they looked up to watch Holly curiously as she mounted the steps and threaded her way through the tables into the cool, dark interior of the building. It took several seconds for her eyes to adjust, and then she saw that there were more tables spread with gay, red-and-white-checked cloths, and a long counter that stretched the width of the room. On it were several glass-fronted cabinets containing weird and wonderful-looking foods that reminded Holly sharply that she hadn't eaten for quite some time.

At the moment the room was empty, but when Holly rang a bell set on the counter, a bead curtain covering a doorway was pushed aside and a stout middle-aged man with a balding head and a walrus mustache came to attend to her. He took one look at her and spoke to her in English.

"Yes, madame. What would you like?"

Holly smiled to herself, wondering whether he had really been able to sum up her nationality so easily, or whether he automatically addressed all foreigners in English.

"I'm looking for somewhere to stay," she told him. "Do you have any rooms here?"

"Oh, yes. We have many nice rooms. How long you want room for?"

She gave a slight shrug. "I'm not sure yet. Definitely for a week, but it could be longer."

"Is no matter. Come, I show you the room."

He lifted up a flap in the counter. Holly left her case in the bar while he led the way through a big kitchen, where a young boy was standing on a box to wash the dishes in a deep sink. The kitchen still smelled enticingly of the meals that had been cooked there at lunchtime. Holly determinedly ignored the noises her stomach was making and followed the man through a door that gave out to the open air again at the side of the *taverna*. A flight of concrete stairs that had pots of brightly colored flowers on either side of every step led up the outside of the building to a blue door that was ajar, opening onto a corridor with rooms on either side of it.

The Greek opened one of the doors on the left-hand side and stood back for her to enter. The room was very plain, with only a wooden double bed and white coverlet, a small wardrobe and ancient chest of drawers, a table and chair. Over in the corner stood a hand basin and a mirror with a crack across the corner. But the place was spotlessly clean and the shutters across the windows made it deliciously cool. During the course of her work Holly had stayed in far worse places. This was a palace compared to the lodging house in India three years ago, and which she still recalled with a shudder of distaste even now. But long experience had taught her always to double-check, so she turned to the hotel keeper and said firmly, "I'd like to see the bathroom, please."

But this, too, proved to be clean, if primitive, and soon Holly had unpacked and was standing in the longed-for shower, feeling the tepid water rinse away her tiredness along with the grime of travel. Refreshed, she put on a pale blue cotton sundress and went along the corridor to stand for a while on the little landing at the top of the steps. Looking out to sea, she could just make out a smudge of darker color on the horizon. Holly wondered if it could be the small island of Fallipos where Felix Riddell lived the life of a recluse, the privately-owned island as securely barred to intruders and casual sightseers as any ancient fortress. But she had come to Greece with the express intention of bearding the lion in his den, and had no intention of leaving until she had done so!

She still felt physically tired, but the shower had helped, so Holly decided not to rest now, but to wait until after dinner and then have an early night. The tavern keeper, who had introduced himself as Alexis Lambis, told her that they would start to serve the evening meals in an hour, so she automatically took one of her smaller cameras from the big shoulder bag and set off to explore the town for a while. At first she turned her steps inland, threading her way through narrow, twisting cobbled streets that seemed to have been built with no plan or purpose. They often went off at a tangent to circle a house that seemed to have been built right across the way, and joined up frequently with other streets. It was easy to become lost, as most of the houses looked exactly the same and only an occasional shop stood out as a landmark. As she went farther inland the road grew progressively steeper, and Holly found walking in her high-heeled sandals difficult because the cobbles were so uneven and slippery. She eventually reached the edge of the town and sat down on a low wall to rest. Just behind her there was an olive grove and the rich oily smell of the wood came strongly to her nostrils from a nearby stack of recently cut logs. She could see two white nanny goats cropping the grass in a nearby field and, distantly, the sound of sheep bells echoed in the hills. The sun was much lower now, the shadows longer, and it was very still and peaceful, so still that you could almost hear the silence. Holly sat there for some time, her thoughts miles away, but then the clatter of hooves roused her from her reverie. She saw a man and a boy driving a herd of about ten heavily laden donkeys down from the hills toward the town. She smiled; now she knew why the cobbles were so slippery; they had been worn smooth by the iron shoes of the donkeys.

The town was much busier as she made her way back; its inhabitants emerged after the long after-noon siesta, all the shop doors were thrown wide open and the streets thronged with people—women with shopping bags, running children, and men who sat at low tables playing backgammon. Inevita-bly she got lost, but kept going downhill and even-tually came out quite a long way to the left of the *taverna* and had to walk back along the harbor past the fishing caïques and the pleasure cruisers. There were more men around now, mending nets on the harbor wall or working on the boats. Holly strolled past, keeping a trained but casual eye open for anything that might make a good photograph. She glanced across at one of the smaller boats and then came to an abrupt stop, her heart jumping in her chest, her mind frozen!

For several agonizing seconds she stood and stared at a man who had briefly come onto the deck of the boat, but then he went below again and Holly began to relax, letting out her suspended breath and giving herself a tremulous mental shake. For a moment there she had thought.... But no, it was really quite unlike him; the man had been much bigger than Nick had, his hair lighter. But the inci-dent had shaken her, for she had thought she was over that sort of thing by now. She began to walk again, hurrying toward the *taverna*. It had happened before, of course, many times, especially at the be-

ginning when the hurt had been raw and bleeding.
She would see a figure in a crowd, a man who held
his head a certain way, or walked with that long,
purposeful stride as if he was really going somewhere, and her heart would do that crazy jerk and
then stand still until she realized with a sick feeling
of bitter disappointment that it wasn't Nick. It had
never been Nick. Since the day he had walked out
after that last terrible row, she had never seen or
heard anything of him again.

Several of the tables at the *taverna* were filled
when she reached it, mostly by Greeks who were
conducting animated discussions over their drinks.
One or two were taken by tourists who recognized
her as one of themselves and nodded to her as she
came in. Holly returned the greetings with a smile
but chose a table by herself on the edge of the terrace, more shaken than she cared to admit and angry with herself for having let such a trivial incident
affect her at all. It had been seven years—seven
long years, and yet just seeing someone who reminded her of Nick could still make her go to
pieces!

Her annoyance increased when she found that
her hands were shaking as she held the menu, but
she managed to give her order to the waiter in a
steady enough voice, and gradually regained her
composure as she tucked into a filling dish of spiced
meat that was completely unpronounceable but
tasted delicious. Afterward she ordered another
coffee and went over her notes on Felix Riddell. In
a nutshell, he was a second generation Canadian of
British descent who had started off as a newspaper

delivery boy from a poor family and had worked his
way up to owning the newspaper group and becoming a millionaire several times over by the time he
was thirty. He had then set out to become one of
the richest men in the world by taking over business empires that fell like ninepins before his ruthless determination. For several years he had been
one of the leaders of the jet-set scene, a playboy
who had gone through three wives and an uncount-
able number of mistresses, until it almost became
unfashionable *not* to have been one or the other.
Then, quite suddenly, Felix Riddell had thrown up
his life-style—the yachts, casinos, women, the
whole thing—left his empire in the hands of under-
lings and bought a remote Greek island where he
had shut himself away. He turned the place into an
impregnable fortress where only the chosen few
were allowed to visit, and those few definitely— *but
definitely*—did not include journalists who wanted to
interview him for a story.

Holly glanced up but could no longer see the island on the horizon. The sun was setting, turning
the sky to a fierce molten crimson that blinded her
to everything but its magnificence. She tried to concentrate on working out her approach to Felix Riddell, if she ever got to see him, but she felt very
tired in that soporific kind of fatigue where it is too
much trouble to even move to go to bed. Gazing at
the sunset, letting herself drown in the glory of
color, Holly gradually let her mind go back to the
thoughts that had been hovering there since the incident earlier, no matter how much she had tried to
ignore them, to bury them in forgetfulness. Back

more than seven years to when she had been six-
teen and still a schoolgirl, and had met a student
called Nicholas Falconer and had fallen instantly,
madly in love with him.

It had been a disaster from the start, of course.
Nick had been only twenty-two and in his last year
at university, where he was taking a degree in civil
engineering. They had met at a disco and at first
Nick had looked on her feelings for him as a phase,
expecting her to grow out of it. He treated her with
a kind of elder-brother kindness and affection that
she neither wanted nor knew how to overcome.
But she'd persevered and one night, when he'd
gone to give her his usual light good-night kiss on
the cheek, she'd turned in his arms and kissed him
properly, and his surprised response had left her in
no doubt that he had at last started to think of her
as a woman.

But even then it hadn't been easy; he'd insisted
that they were too young, that he had still to find a
job, and it would be years before he would be making enough money to support a wife. To Holly his
arguments and reservations were nonsense. They
loved each other, didn't they? So what was the
point of waiting? Gradually she had worn him
down and at last, against his better judgment, he
gave in—perhaps because he was an orphan and
longed for a home life of his own, perhaps because
he realized just how desperately Holly loved and
wanted him, and that if they didn't marry soon they
might not be able to control their emotions for
much longer.

Holly's parents could, she supposed, be regarded

as upper middle class; they had sent her to good schools and had great ambitions for her, their only daughter. When Holly introduced them to Nick and told them they wanted to get married, they were incredibly shocked, looking on Nick as a sponger and forbidding him to enter the house. At first she had been stunned by their attitude; to her Nick was perfect and she was so besotted by him that it had never occurred to her that her parents might object. The stubborn streak that had been part of her nature since childhood, and that often stood her in good stead in her job now, had helped her to gradually wear them down, until at last they capitulated and said that if she would agree not to see Nick for several months until he'd taken his exams, and if they afterward still felt the same, they would allow them to become engaged. This, of course, in the firm conviction that by then Holly would have got over her infatuation for him.

Holly acceded to this readily enough, knowing that Nick wanted time to concentrate on his studies anyway, even though being apart from him was a bittersweet kind of pain as the months dragged by. She marked each day off on the calendar, longing for the time to pass. On the day after his last exam she took the train to Oxford and he was waiting at the station to meet her. He looked so very dear; tall and youthfully slim—too thin for his height, really— his thick brown hair falling forward over his forehead, and his blue eyes lighting up as he caught sight of her and ran to meet her.

They grabbed each other and hugged and kissed

exuberantly, regardless of the other passengers who walked past them, grinning broadly.

Nick picked her up and swung her around excitedly. "Guess what? I've been offered a job!"

"A job! Oh, Nick, how marvelous. Now daddy won't be able to have the least objection to our getting married." She kissed him fervently, hugging him tightly. "What sort of job? When do you start?"

He laughed and set her down, then flushed as he realized that people were looking at them in amusement. Grabbing her hand he began to hurry her along. "Come on, let's find somewhere we can eat, and I'll tell you all about it."

They found a nearby café, and over coffee and sticky buns, he told her, "It's with a big international construction company. They've offered me a post at the very lowest of their junior management levels, but at least it's a start and it's heading in the direction I want to go," he added enthusiastically. "I went for an interview last month, and I heard that I'd been accepted only this week. They have construction sites all over the world." His eyes lighted up eagerly. "Just think, I could be sent to South America one year, Africa the next."

Holly's eyes widened in alarm. "You will be able to take me with you, won't you?"

He began to frown and said slowly, "Well, I'm afraid . . . ."

She reached out and clutched at his hand in alarm, almost knocking over her cup of coffee in her haste. "Oh, Nick, you can't go without me.

Please, please, say you won't go without me!"

His face softened and he gave her the special
smile he had for no one else. He lifted his other
hand to cover hers. "Idiot, I was only teasing. Of
course I can take you with me; it was one of the first
things I asked."

Holly gave a shudder of relief, then said earnestly, "Don't tease me like that again, Nick. Promise me you won't? I can't bear it."

He lifted a long finger to wipe away a tear that
had appeared on her cheek and said softly, using his
pet name for her, "Silly young Prickles. Don't you
know I won't ever leave you?"

That memory brought a wry, twisted smile to
Holly's face. So much for promises. For he had left
her such a short time later.

Hindsight had shown her that it had been entirely
her parents' fault. When they had heard about
Nick's job they had refused point-blank to let her
marry at once and go slumming around the world
with him, as they expressed it. They hadn't brought
up their daughter to live among a lot of foreign
workmen on a primitive building site without decent sanitation or medical care. And when Holly
had stubbornly said that she was going anyway,
they had pointed out that she was still under eigh-
teen and unable to marry without their consent.
There had been tears, recriminations and angry
scenes, and in the end a compromise was reached
only when Holly threatened to leave home and go
to live with Nick if they wouldn't let them get married at once. They agreed to let them marry only if
Nick gave up the job with the construction com-

pany and agreed to take a post in her father's business, working in the office.

The condition was completely opposite to what they wanted, but Holly's father had taken Nick to his club and told him that Holly was a delicately brought-up girl who would not be able to stand the rigors of living in a foreign climate, and that if Nick loved her he would not ask her to make such a sacrifice. Her father was eloquent and persuasive and Nick young and unsure, so that he eventually agreed to give up his ambitions and to take the job with her father. Pressing home his advantage, Mr. Weston had no compunction in pointing out to Nick that he was in no position to provide a decent home for Holly, who couldn't possibly be expected to live in some tiny apartment or squalid bed-sitter where she would be ashamed to entertain her family and friends, and that it would be only sensible for them to live with her parents in the family home until such time as Nick could afford a house.

Nick, made to feel inferior and ashamed of his lack of background and money, and his apparent disregard for Holly's comfort, reluctantly agreed. Holly, when she was told of it, felt only a pang of disappointment; it would have been fun to have lived abroad and to have had their own place to live in, but all that really mattered to her was that she was going to marry Nick right away. She was so in love that she was incapable of seeing beyond that glorious moment. Once they were married everything would work out and be wonderful because they would be together. Nothing could change that.

They had had a large, white wedding, insisted on

and paid for by her parents, and went on honeymoon to a villa in Spain loaned by her aunt, an ecstatic time that had left everlasting memories of love, happiness and discovery, when there seemed to be just the two of them in a beautiful world that was all their own.

Her parents' campaign to break them up had started from the moment they returned. Oh, it had been very subtle, of course, and conducted in an extremely polite manner, so that Holly hadn't even realized it was happening until it was too late. Her mother especially had been overtly pleasant enough to Nick, but had insinuatingly let him know that he was not one of them, that his social manners left much to be desired. She did it in sentences that began, "I'm sure you won't mind me advising you, Nicholas, but..." or "That isn't *quite* the way we do things, Nicholas." While at work he was relegated to being just an office boy without being given any opportunity to use his brain or to train for management. He was also in the invidious position of being resented by his fellow clerks because he was the boss's son-in-law, while those already at management level were jealous and wary because they thought he was after their jobs.

Nick must have been bitterly unhappy, but he said nothing to Holly, learning fast and making sure that he never made the same mistake twice, and at first Holly was so happy that she never even noticed. But then even their sex life, which before had been so wonderful, so perfect, began to be affected; this because, one morning at breakfast, her mother had complained, politely, of course, of the noise they had made during a bedtime romp when Nick had chased her around the room the night before.

From that moment Nick seemed to withdraw into a shell, gradually losing the spontaneous gaiety and zest for living that she loved. He had begged her then to leave her parents' house and find an apartment somewhere, his words urgent, desperate almost. But Holly was completely blind to what he was going through, unable to see why he would want to leave a comfortable home for a dingy bed-sitter, especially when she was having such a wonderful time showing off her new husband to all her friends. They were invited out often to parties, discos and barbecues, and Holly was engrossed in the enjoyment of no longer being a schoolgirl, of being a married woman and able to do more or less as she liked.

Nick had changed toward her then, treating her as he did her parents; with polite coldness, as if he were a lodger in the house and not a member of the family. And he made love to her only infrequently, when her parents were out of the house, until even this ceased altogether. The quarrels had started then. Holly, unable to understand why he had changed so much when he had been so passionate, so demanding during their honeymoon, and Nick bitter and resentful at her lack of understanding, made on all sides to feel inadequate and inferior. At first they had made up quite quickly after their fights, Holly tearful and repentant, Nick gentle and loving, but things had quickly got worse, the rows fiercer, the insults barbed and hurtful.

The last unforgettable row had taken place almost exactly six months after their marriage. Nick had tried to please her mother by spending a weekend carefully and painstakingly decorating a room for her, and then came home from the office the next day to find a hired man redoing it while her mother stood there with a friend and laughed at Nick's "feeble clumsiness." Unable to stand any more, he had told Holly to start packing, that they were leaving, but she was still too young and inexperienced to see that he had been pushed over the edge at last and told him he was being stupid.

The quarrel then had been terrible, each hurling abuse and insults at the other. Nick demanded that she choose between her parents and him, while Holly refused to do any such thing, and shouted that he was selfish and a fool.

"And an impotent one at that!" she yelled at him, all the hurt and misery of the nights when he had laid stiff and cold beside her flooding into her accusation.

Something seemed to have exploded inside Nick then. He had leaped across the room at her, grabbing her and dragging her toward the bed. Holly saw the look of murderous rage in his eyes and started to struggle, but he overpowered her with a brutality that he had never shown before and threw her down on the bed. Holly screamed, but her parents had gone out to dinner and there was no one to hear her cries as he began to tear off her clothes.

His voice shaking with anger and emotion, he said through clenched teeth, "You bitch! I'll show you whether or not I'm impotent!" And then he had taken her cruelly like an animal, with neither love nor passion, using her body as a means of useless retaliation for all the punishment he had taken.

Afterward she had pulled the sheet over herself and lain, naked and crying, while he had packed his things and walked out of the room, out of her life, sitting up to call his name when it was too late, when he had already gone.

She had waited then, waited for nearly six long, grim weeks, her confidence that he loved her enough to phone her or come for her gradually diminishing as time passed. There had been nothing, not even a letter. It seemed to her afterward that she had grown up in those six weeks, changed from a girl living in a beautiful dream to a woman facing the harsh realities of desertion and loneliness. At the end of that time, her eyes completely opened to what her parents had done, she had left their house for good, only staying on that long in the hope that Nick would contact her. When she left they accused her of ingratitude and heartlessness and told her they never wanted to see her again. Whether they really meant it or not, Holly didn't know, or care very much. She had broken with them completely and didn't even know where they were living, now that they had moved away from the family home. She had grimly set about building a new life for herself, reverting to her maiden name and living in a seedy bed-sitter in a shabby, dilapidated old house while she tried to get a job, any job, and went to evening classes for journalism. It had been hard at first, desperately hard, and she often thought that she couldn't cope, that it would be better just to feed the gas meter with all the money she had left and leave the taps open, but the stubborn streak that had made her fight to marry Nick had made her carry on somehow, to overcome the desolation and loneliness, the continued exhaustion and frequent periods when she was weak from hunger because her unemployment money had run out.

But then Jamie had come into her life, and life had suddenly seemed worth living again when there were two of them to fight for.

The thought of Jamie made her remember how he had looked when she had left him the previous morning, emerging from sleep, his hair disheveled, to hold her tightly and kiss her goodbye, his long-lashed blue eyes filled with love. Holly blinked rapidly, having hated to leave him behind when she was given an assignment abroad, and longing to be back with him.

She sighed, then gave a resigned shrug; once more becoming aware of her surroundings as a waiter came to place a glass bowl with a candle in it on her table. It was dark now, the sun having set completely while she was deep in her memories of the past. The lamps had been lighted along the quay, and out at sea she could see the lights of the fishing boats bobbing gently on the slight tide. Several of the boats tied up at the harbor also had light shafting from portholes and windows in the cabins, the larger ones even having gay strings of colored lights outlining the rigging, giving them a fairylike appearance.

As Holly looked at the boats she noticed the man who had given her such a start earlier come on deck again and stand silhouetted for a moment by the riding light fixed to the mast of his boat. Then he turned to jump athletically onto the quay and stroll leisurely toward the *taverna*. As he came nearer, passing through the pools of light thrown by the electric lamps, she could see him more clearly. He was over six feet tall, the same height as Nick had been, but much broader. His muscles and strong chest were outlined by the navy sweater he wore, the sleeves were pushed up, and his hands were thrust casually into the pockets of his jeans. And he was far more assured, carried himself with a commanding air of self-confidence that Nick had never had, as if he was used to giving orders and being obeyed. Another stretch of darkness until the next light, and now she could see his face quite well as he looked toward the *taverna*. The man's hair was thick and looked dark, although it was difficult to tell in the artificial light, and one lock fell a little forward onto his forehead. After the last patch of darkness he was climbing the steps to the *taverna* and stood at the entrance to the terrace, looking around. He was deeply tanned, as if he had been living in a sunny climate for a long time. About thirty, his face was very strong, with a square jaw and high cheekbones, and a scar that ran across his left temple to his eyebrow gave him an almost satanical appearance. His mouth was thin, with a cynical twist to it, and there was a withdrawn look about his eyes, eyes that were a startling blue, as blue as the summer sky.

He walked forward and stopped in front of her table. The remembered picture of the youth she had married disintegrated as Nick, the man, said calmly, "Hello, Holly. How are you?"

CHAPTER TWO

STRANGELY, HOLLY WAS ABLE to return his greeting almost as calmly, the second shock canceling out the first and leaving her completely emotionless, almost in a state of limbo.

"Hello, Nick. I'm fine. And you?" But before he could answer, she added with a small smile, "But I hardly need ask, need I? You look extremely fit."

His left eyebrow, the one arched by the scar, rose a fraction as if he was surprised by her lack of reaction. He gave a slight nod of acknowledgment and took his hand out of his pocket to put it on the back of the chair opposite. "May I join you?"

"Of course."

He sat down, blocking out the sea.

For a moment he studied her intently, but then the waiter came up and he looked away. "Would you like a drink?"

Holly didn't want to drink with him—she wanted to run to her room, to shut the door and hide—but she managed to shrug and say offhandedly, "Why not? A vodka and tonic, please."

Nick's brows flickered a little. "A very sophisticated drink."

Her tone hardening, Holly said tartly, "I'm an adult, not a schoolgirl anymore."

The blue eyes came up to meet hers. "So I see." Then, he added abruptly, "You've changed."

She nodded. "So have you. I hardly recognized you."

The cynical twist of his mouth deepened for a moment. "That wasn't quite what I meant." His eyes ran over her face, feature by feature, leaving her feeling strangely naked and vulnerable. "I would always have known you. You look just as I remember you the last time I saw you."

Glad of the semidarkness that hid the flush that came to her cheeks as she remembered the circumstances of their last meeting, she said in defensive sarcasm, "Next you'll be trotting out the trite adage that seven years is a long time."

Nick looked at her swiftly and seemed about to make a retort, but the waiter appeared with their drinks. He picked his up and leaned back in his chair, crossing his legs negligently, his tone calm again.

"What brings you to Kinos?"

"Business," she replied shortly, and then because he waited, his eyebrow raised inquiringly, she added, "I'm on an assignment here."

"Assignment?"

"For a paper. I'm a journalist," she told him reluctantly.

But to her surprise he showed no reaction, merely giving a brief nod.

"And you?" she asked him. "What are you doing here?"

"Oh, mine's purely a pleasure trip." He gestured toward the boat. "I've hired a motor yacht and I'm taking a leisurely sail around the Greek islands, just stopping where I feel like it.''

"How very pleasant." Holly felt oddly detached, as if it wasn't really her that was sitting here making polite conversation. Picking up her glass she took a long drink. Suddenly her hand began to shake, almost spilling the liquid. Hastily she set the glass down and put her hands under the table, clasping them together. The numbness had gone and her heart began to hammer in her chest. What was she doing here, drinking and exchanging trivialities with a man who had walked out on her and hadn't even cared enough to find out how she was, whether she was alive, even, in the period since? Her voice uneven, she said, "Have you been here long?"

Thankfully Nick didn't seem to notice anything amiss. "No, not very long. I haven't seen you here before, and as this is almost the only place to stay, I presume you only arrived today?"

She nodded woodenly. "Yes, on this afternoon's ferry." Then she screwed up her courage to ask the one all-important question. "I expect you'll be moving on quite soon, then?"

His lids came down swiftly over his eyes like a camera shutter. His face expressionless, he said evenly, "I've made no definite plans. I may stick around here for a while."

"I see."

His brows rose. "My being here doesn't bother you, does it?"

Holly laughed harshly. "Why should it?" She added deliberately, "You're nothing to me now."

His blue eyes were suddenly cold as glacier ice as they came up to meet her gray ones. "Was I ever?"

For a long moment Holly could only stare at him speechlessly, then, unable to stand the situation any longer, she got abruptly to her feet and said hastily, "I'm very tired from the journey. You'll have to excuse me. Good night."

Nick stood up to let her go by and her arm brushed against his as she passed. It was as if an electric shock had scorched through her body, leaving every nerve raw and tingling. He said goodnight in return, but Holly kept her face averted as she hurried down the terrace steps and along to the outside stairs leading to her room, not stopping until she was inside with the door firmly locked behind her. Then she almost collapsed onto the bed, her whole body shivering uncontrollably as if she was very cold.

Holly hadn't bothered to turn on the light, and she lay for so long in the darkness that the moon came out and shafted through the windows, lighting her as she huddled on the bed hugging herself to try and stop the violent tremors that only gradually subsided. From below her room, on the terrace, she could hear the noise of voices talking, some raised in laughter, as the locals came along for their evening drinks, and then the taped sound of bouzouki music floated up from the bar, tinny and garishly unlike the real thing. Slowly she got up and went to stand at her window, gently pushing open the shutters so that she could look out. The lights of the fishing boats were far out to sea now, bobbing about like fairy lights in the wind. Tentatively Holly

looked down toward the terrace, wondering if Nick
was still there, but the thickness of the vine covered
the area almost completely, leaving only one or two
patches where it was possible to glimpse the metal
tables and the people sitting around them. Lifting
her eyes, she sought his boat among those moored
at the quay, but it was difficult to tell them apart in
the darkness—they were just a jumble of darker
spars reaching up into the blackness of the night.

She drew back into the room and leaned against
the wall. Why did Nick have to be here? Why? She
had imagined this moment so often, had had night-
mares about it for years, knowing that eventually it
must come, but she had never thought it would be
like this—purely by chance in a foreign country.
She had always imagined that it would be in a law
court or lawyer's office when she would have had
plenty of time to prepare herself, to be completely
self-controlled and able to deal with the situation.
But this—this had shaken her badly, more than she
cared to admit, shattering the hard shell she had
built around herself over the years into tiny frag-
ments that would have to be painfully put back together before she could face him again.

She shivered and rubbed her bare arms, pacing
up and down the small room. She supposed that it
was inevitable that she would see him again. Kinos
was such a small place, and Melmia the only town,
that anyone staying there must of necessity bump
into each other a dozen times a day. Holly smiled
cynically to herself; the malignant fate that had
brought him to Kinos at the same time as she

wasn't going to let her off the hook as easily as just one short encounter. The knife was bound to be twisted deeper before it let her go.

Closing the shutters, she turned on the light and began to slowly undress and get ready for bed, although she knew that it would be a long time before she would sleep tonight. Her thoughts went back to Jamie waiting for her in England, and although she tried not to, she immediately began comparing him with Nick, their two faces chasing each other through her thoughts. A slow tear trickled down her cheek and Holly brushed it angrily away. She hadn't cried over Nick for a long time now, and she certainly didn't intend to start just because he'd come back into her life. What the hell was there to cry about, anyway? She should be glad that she'd got the chance to see him again and to know that she'd got him out of her hair for good. And the tears? They were pure nostalgia, for a brief period of happiness when she'd been young and incredibly stupid. They certainly weren't self-pity for the woman she'd become, or for regret at what might have been. She had Jamie and she had her job; she was completely independent financially and had no other emotional ties—and wanted none. Her life was complete and this unexpected meeting with Nick could be looked on as merely a rather unpleasant interlude that would soon be over and done with, she told herself forcefully. It might even turn out to be therapeutic, laying to rest many old ghosts that had haunted her for years after he had gone. But she must be careful not to mention

Jamie; *that* relationship was too precious to be made known to the man who had once lived with her as her husband.

The noise from the *taverna* below began to die away until all was quiet. The town slept peacefully while Holly still stirred restlessly on the strange, rather lumpy mattress, but gradually the years of self-discipline, when she had had to force herself to overcome so many torments and difficulties, began to extend their influence and she lay more quietly, feeling herself better able to cope with seeing Nick again. But her last waking thought before she at last drifted off to sleep was that he looked so different—had changed so much.

Sunlight shafted through the louvered shutters the next morning, making golden bars of light across the bed and the floor. One reached Holly's eyes, making her blink and turn her head away as she slowly came out of sleep. For a moment she lay languidly, her mind still lost in the fog of unconsciousness, unaware of where she was, thinking that she was in the big bed in the cottage at home, waiting for Jamie to wake her with his usual morning kiss. Her eyes flickered open, taking in the white-washed ceiling, the roughly plastered walls painted pale blue like the color of Nick's eyes ....

Holly came instantly wide awake, trembling, fully aware of her surroundings.

It took a great deal of courage to leave her room that morning, but she determinedly ran down the flight of stairs between the tubs of deep red geraniums and pink and white carnations, the scent of the flowers coming up to surround her as she descended. And when she reached the ground she saw that she needn't have worried; Nick's boat was gone from its mooring, leaving a space among the boats like the gap where a tooth had been pulled. Relief flooded her; he must have decided to leave after all, not to hang around and have old memories rise up from their graves and resurrect their grizzled heads. But as she mounted the terrace steps she saw his boat tacking toward the harbor, its russet sails set to catch the sea breeze. He had only been out fishing.

The proprietor himself brought her breakfast of rolls and coffee, and Holly took the opportunity of booking two calls to England, expecting to have to wait some time for the connections, but was pleasantly surprised when he told her that the island had just had a new exchange installed and there would only be about an hour's delay. Holly spent the time exploring the little shops nearby, which luckily hadn't yet become the usual store of rather tawdry mass-produced souvenirs for tourists. What items of Greek traditional work they had were mostly made on the island by the inhabitants in their spare time. Holly reached up to admire beautifully embroidered blouses and dresses suspended on poles attached to the shop awnings, and was envious of the patience that had gone into making delicate lacework tablecloths and napkins. She bought a straw hat, knowing from past experience of hot climates how much damage the sun did to her fair hair, bleaching it almost silver if exposed to it for too long.

At ten she went back to the hotel and sat on the

terrace with a cool drink until Alexis Lambis called her in to take the first of her calls.

The familiar voice of the Features editor greeted her and then got down to business straightaway.

"Still no definite word on the interview with Felix Riddell yet, Holly. As you know, we're still waiting for one of his employees to fix it for us. The last word we had was that Riddell was on the point of agreeing, so stay on hand so that you can get there fast when he does make up his mind. We don't want to give him time to change it," he added fervently. "It's taken enough persuasion and bribes to get this far. Have you fixed up somewhere to stay?"

"Yes, it's the Taverna Helios," Holly told him, and gave him the phone number.

"Okay. You'd better stick within spitting distance of the phone today, but I'll give you a call at five this evening our time, anyway, to give you the latest information. Can't have you sitting around in luxury doing nothing for too long or I'll have the editor after me," he added with mock severity.

Holly laughed. "If you call this luxury, then just don't give me any assignments to any lesser places."

She put down the receiver and left the cool shade of the building to sit out in the sun again and wait for her second call to come through, the really important call. To Jamie. Jamie, oh, Jamie! Her thoughts clung to him like a drowning person clings to a spar. He was her reason for being, for existing. Without him she would have gone under long ago. She needed him, the reassurance of knowing he was there, waiting for her, the center of his world. Because it was that reassurance, and only that, that would give her the courage and steadfastness to face seeing Nick again.

The phone rang, its strident tones cutting through the still air and Holly reached it almost before Lambis did. He spoke in Greek to the operator, then smiled at Holly. "It is for you, *thespoinis*," he said, holding out the receiver.

Holly took it, her hand shaking. "Jamie?"

But it was Mrs. Ferrers, the housekeeper, who answered, and she had to wait again before Jamie came on.

"Mummy!" His six-year-old voice piped shrilly across the line. "I'm digging a hole in the garden so that rabbits will come and live there. Can I have a rabbit, please? As soon as you come home?"

"But you've already got the guinea pigs and a hamster," Holly answered in useless protest, knowing that she would give in to him.

He went chattering on, her little son, telling her of his day at school yesterday, of a broken toy; all the little things that were of supreme importance in his young life, and suddenly all Holly's anxiety disappeared; she was right when she had told Nick that he was nothing to her now; his child, whom he didn't even know existed, had completely taken his place.

Happiness filled her as she talked. The ghost had indeed been laid, and she was ready to face Nick now with perfect composure, as a man she had once known well but who didn't matter anymore.

The sun beckoned after she had finished the call and she hurried up to her room to change into a swimsuit, humming a tune as she did so. Going to the mirror to rub suntan lotion on her face and freshen up her lipstick, she was annoyed to see the dark shadows around her eyes from the sleepless night. That would never do. Still, when in Greece, one wears sunglasses! Holly perched the large round-framed specs on her nose, stuffed a bag with the usual beach paraphernalia and went to find a quiet place to sun herself.

She found it a couple of hundred yards away from the harbor and the town after scrambling over rocks worn smooth and slippery by the sea, and little inlets of shingle, the washed stones bright and sparkling in the sun. Beyond the rocks there was a cove of fine, golden sand surrounded by quite high cliffs. The beach shelved gently to the water except where arms of rock jutted out to the sea, providing ideal platforms from which to dive.

It was too much to hope for to have the place to herself, of course—she had guessed that when she had asked the hotel proprietor for the nearest beach and he had immediately directed her here. There was a young couple farther along that she remembered having seen eating a meal in the *taverna* last night and whom she guessed to be Scandinavians from their appearance, and, on loungers set under a huge sunshade, lay a group of people, including two very tanned women, looking extremely rich and pampered even though they were only dressed in the merest wisps of material. Off one of the big yachts, Holly guessed. One or two Greek children played by the waterline, but there were no other islanders sunning themselves—they were all so naturally brown that they had no need to.

Holly spread her towel out on the sand and slipped

out of her sundress, rolling it up to make a pillow. She reached up to clip her hair up at the back before she went into the water, her body tall and slender in a dusty pink bikini, her legs long and shapely. The water struck cold at first, the sea dragging the sand back around her feet, burying them like quicksand, but as she went deeper and then dipped her shoulders underwater, it wrapped around her like a warm blanket, unbelievably soft and caressing. And blue, so blue and clear; she could look down and see her feet through the water, and the patches of darker seaweed that clung to the few sand-covered rocks on the shelving bottom. She let the swell pick her up and struck out toward the open sea in a strong, regular crawl, her arms clearing the water cleanly. After a while she stopped to tread water, out of breath but feeling fresh and invigorated. It had been quite some time since she had had an opportunity to swim, although she had done so regularly when she'd been at school and had even won several medals for it. But that had been before Nick, of course. And after he had left her there had been Jamie to look after and the constant fight to keep them both, with no time for swimming, no time for anything except work and exhausted sleep at the end of the day.

Rolling over, Holly lay back and floated, wondering idly if this was what a water bed was like, and thinking that she must give Jamie swimming lessons when she got back to England—he was old enough now. Conceived during that last terrible quarrel, when Nick had taken her so violently, one might perhaps expect that Jamie would be an emotional, bad-tempered child. But he wasn't—he was happy as the day was long, only sad when she had to leave him with someone else. And that had happened often when he was a baby and had to be left with baby-sitters or in a day nursery while Holly worked or went to classes in journalism and photography. But he'd been so brave, blinking back his tears and seeming to understand that she couldn't help it—and running to her, clinging, clinging so tightly when she came back, as if he'd been secretly afraid that she never would. But it had paid off in the end; she had managed to get a job on a magazine as a photojournalist, and after a few years she got her present position with a good national newspaper where her feature stories appeared often in their Sunday color supplement. It had enabled her to buy the cottage tucked away in a fold of the English countryside with a garden for Jamie to play in, and to pay a housekeeper she could trust to look after him when she was sent on an assignment, although she mostly tried to restrict these to as near home as possible now. But this one, and the chance of getting an interview with Felix Riddell, had been irresistible.

She turned and swam back to the shore, lazily now, taking her time and enjoying the feel of the sun on her back and the rainbow of colors in the drops of water that fell like crystal when she deliberately splashed her hand against the waves. Not bothering to dry herself, Holly lay facedown on her towel and almost instantly fell asleep.

Some sixth sense brought her fully awake almost as soon as the shadow touched her. She had been dreaming, and when she turned over and looked up to see Nick standing over her, his hands on his hips, it came as no surprise to see him there, and she realized her dream must have been about him. Quickly she sat up and reached for her sunglasses, feeling deeply grateful for being able to hide behind them.

Nick dropped down to the sand beside her, facing her. Dressed only in a T-shirt and pale blue shorts, he half lay on the sand, his legs, brown and firm as tree trunks, stretched out alongside hers. Holly immediately swung her legs to one side, then remembered the straw hat and put it on, further shading her eyes.

There was a thin smile on Nick's lips as he said, "Does the sun hurt your eyes?"

"I find the reflection of it on the sea rather dazzling," Holly returned calmly, adding rather pointedly, "Have you come for a swim?"

"That was the general idea." He leaned back on his elbows. "But I've just had lunch. Have to give it an hour or so first. Here, I've brought you a present." He fished in his pocket and brought out an apple, green and hard, with just a flush of red near the crown. He held it out to her.

Holly looked at it without moving, then raised her eyes to find him watching her quizzically.

"The serpent won't bite you if you take it," he said softly, mockingly.

Reaching out, Holly took the apple, being careful not to let her fingers touch his. "How did you know I was here?"

"Alexis Lambis told me."

She looked up quickly. "There hasn't been a phone call for me, has there?"

Nick's brows rose. "No. Were you expecting one?"

She nodded silently, eating the apple.

"Something to do with your assignment here?"

"Something like that," she agreed shortly.

"Isn't this rather an out-of-the-way place for a journalist to be sent for a story?"

"Some people might think so."

"Which means that you're not going to tell me about it, I suppose?"

"That's right. In other words, mind your own business," Holly said caustically.

"Tut, tut. Still as prickly as ever, I see," Nick returned, a cold edge of irony in his voice.

Holly's head came up sharply and for a long moment their glances held, until she turned away and pulled her knees up to rest her chin on them.

Nick took a pack of cigarettes from his shirt pocket and lighted one while Holly dug a hole and buried the apple core.

They sat silently for some time, each lost in their own thoughts, but then Nick showed how closely parallel his thoughts had been to hers by saying abruptly, "Why did you never get a divorce?"

Holly picked up a handful of sand and let it sift through her fingers, her whole attention absorbed in it. "Why didn't you?" she countered.

To her surprise he laughed, the sound echoing in the bay and attracting the attention of the party from the yacht. "Just like a woman to answer a question with a question. I've never known one yet who would give you a direct answer to a leading question."

She stopped playing with the sand and lifted her head to look at him. "You sound as if you've known a lot of women."

His jaw thrust forward. "Did you expect me to live like a monk just because I was still technically married to you?" he demanded harshly.

Holly stared at him for a moment, startled by his vehemence, then looked away. "I really hadn't thought about it," she said stiffly.

Just then the men from the yacht party walked by them to the sea and began to swim around, noisily throwing a big yellow beach ball to one another. Nick reached up to pull off his shirt, but he made no attempt to go in to swim. He looked very powerful, his chest broad and muscular, but his hips in the washed-out denim shorts looked lean and athletic, as if he got a lot of exercise. He glanced up and caught her watching him.

"You look very tanned," Holly said hastily. "You must have been sailing around the islands for some time."

Shaking his head, Nick said, "No, I've only been in Greece for quite a short time. I got this out in Australia while I was working."

"You live in Australia?"

"No. I was there for a couple of years, building a bridge. And before that in Africa, working on a dam."

"So you got to achieve your ambition and become a civil engineer, after all?"

"Yes, I managed to persuade the company that had offered me a job earlier to take me on after—" he hesitated "—after we split up."

Holly laughed gratingly. "Let's get it right, shall we? You mean after you walked out."

Nick stubbed out his cigarette viciously and leaned toward her, his eyes cold. "No, let's *really* get it right. You were offered a choice, remember? Your parents or me. Well, you made your choice, and in my book you did the deserting bit, not me."

"Well, really!" Holly opened her mouth to argue with him but was interrupted by a trill of laughter coming from the women behind them.

Nick glanced toward them, and then she saw his eyebrows go up, an arrested expression on his face. Holly turned around and saw what had attracted his attention; the two women were sunbathing topless and the laughter had been a deliberate lure to gain Nick's interest, because one of the women was openly smiling at him. Then she got up and came across the beach toward them, walking slowly, her hips swaying. She wore only the smallest possible triangles of material fastened with strings at the sides, but she had gold chains dangling from every conceivable place; around her waist and her ankle, as well as on her wrist and around her neck. She was in her mid thirties, Holly guessed, although it was hard to tell through all the gold eyeshadow and orange lipstick, her hair dyed silver blond and falling into a beautifully cut bell around her head. She exuded money, even before Holly got a whiff of the Jean Pateu perfume.

Completely ignoring Holly as if she wasn't there, the woman came to a stop and stood over Nick, who leaned back on one elbow, looking up at her lazily through half-closed lids, then she slowly lowered herself to her knees in front of him, her jutting, naked breasts only a few inches away from his chest. "Excuse me," she said, her accent definitely French, "but do you 'ave a light, M'sieu?" And she held out a cigarette toward him.

"Of course." Nick sat up and took a lighter from his pocket, cupping the flame for her and letting his eyes meet hers over it, his left eyebrow raised a fraction.

The woman put her hands over his as she bent with the cigarette in her mouth, then she sat back gracefully on her heels and smiled at him brilliantly. "Thank you, m'sieu." Then she added, "Didn't I see you on a boat in the 'arbor?"

Nick nodded. "That's right, the *Argosy*."

"We also are on a sailing holiday." She looked at him seductively. "Our boat is called *Mignette*. You must come and have a drink with us, M'sieu ... ?"

"Falconer," Nick supplied. "Nick Falconer."

"And I am Chantel D'Anneau." She shifted her weight so that she was leaning on one arm, the arm nearest Nick, of course. "You will come for a drink?"

"I'd like to."

"*Bien*. Tonight, at eight, then?"

"Thank you." Nick watched her as she rose to her feet, her breast just happening to catch his arm as she moved. His mouth twisted into a thin smile. "And may I bring my wife?"

For a moment the poise slipped and surprise and then anger showed in the woman's face, but then she recovered and she looked at Holly with a smile that managed to be polite and yet disparaging at the same time. "By all means bring your wife ... if you wish to," she added after a disdainful pause. Then she turned and gave Nick the full benefit of her very curvaceous back view as she rejoined her friend.

Holly looked out to sea at the men playing ball, and said casually, "You'd think with all those gold chains she'd be able to afford a lighter."

Nick grinned. "Cat!" He rolled over onto his elbows as he, too, watched the men. "I wonder which poor sod she's married to?"

Getting quickly to her feet, Holly said, "I think I'll have another swim," and began to walk down toward the sea without looking at him. There had been a bitter edge of cynicism in Nick's voice when he made that last remark, as if he despised all women. She began to wade through the shallows, disturbed suddenly, wondering if it was she who had made him feel like that, had laid the first stone of disillusionment with her sex. She looked back and saw that he was stripping off his shorts to join her in the water. He had on a pair of white trunks underneath and she saw him now as the French woman had seen him; a tall, handsome man, with a strong and beautifully proportioned body; a man with a dominant masculinity that would physically attract any woman. Turning, she plunged into the sea and began to swim, her mind filled with the way he had said "my wife." He had meant it only as a snub for the other woman, she knew, but it made her remember the way he had used to say it when they were first married—with such pride and possessiveness, as if she was the most precious thing in his life.

He was alongside her suddenly, cleaving through the water with his powerful muscles, swimming much better than she remembered. Ignoring him, Holly struck out for the rocks at the side of the cove that stuck out into the sea like giant stepping-stones to nowhere. Reaching one of the farthest rocks, she grabbed hold of the edge and waited for the swell to lift her and help her climb onto its flat surface, but then she felt Nick's hands on her hips as he lifted her bodily out of the water and deposited her on the rock. One thrust of his arms and he had surged out of the sea to join her. Like Neptune rising from the waves, she thought inconsequentially.

But that she had even made the comparison annoyed her, and she said coldly, "I could have managed perfectly well on my own."

Nick glanced at her as he put his hands up to push his wet hair off his face. His mouth twisted wryly but he didn't bother to answer. He seemed to tower over her, rivulets of water running down his smooth chest. His brief trunks had slipped a little and clung to him wetly. Holly got that far and hastily looked away, her heart beating faster suddenly.

"You swim very well now," she said quickly, too quickly.

"I had plenty of practice in Australia." His voice sounded amused as he sat down beside her. "We used to go surfing a lot."

"We?"

"Some of the men I worked with," he supplied, still sounding as if he was laughing inwardly. "We used to go down to the coast nearly every weekend. Some of the beaches there have the best surf in the world."

"And that's all you did—surf?" she asked, letting disbelief show in her tone.

He turned to look at her. "What do you mean?"

Her eyes met his disparagingly; she was angry at herself for being embarrassed and wanted to take it out on him. "Well, you must have found some time in which to get all the experience with women you boasted about earlier."

The blue eyes grew cold and he reached out to catch hold of her wrist, jerking her around to face him. "Don't try and make me out as some sort of sex-crazy lecher. I've had women, yes, and I intend to have plenty more before I'm through." He laughed jeeringly. "Don't tell me that there haven't been other men in your life during the last seven years?"

Holly snatched her wrist away and stood up, glaring down at him furiously. "You're quite right, there have been other men in my life, dozens of them. And even the least of them was a whole lot better in bed than you ever were!"

Then she dived off the rock into the water, but even as she did so she heard his laugh, full and masculine, ring out behind her.

Back on the beach, Holly hurriedly dabbed herself dry, but when she looked back at the rocks she saw that Nick was still there, stretched out in the sun, his head turned away. Slipping the sundress over her head, she gathered up the rest of her gear and started back for the hotel. The Frenchwoman gave her a speculative look as she passed, and when Holly reached the shingle path leading to the harbor, she saw that the woman had already covered her hair with a flower-bedecked bathing cap and was starting to swim toward Nick's rock.

Holly smiled cynically to herself. The woman must really be hard up if she could go back for more after the snub Nick had given her. But perhaps she thought she might be luckier now that he was alone. The shingle gave way to harder ground covered with wild ice daisies, the plant English gardeners called mesembryanthemums, their pretty pink faces wide open to the midday sun. Holly kicked with her sandaled feet at a pebble, but the pain to her toe made her stop short. What was she getting so riled up about? It was nothing to her if Nick made love to every woman in Kinos, was it? No—amend that—had sex with every woman in Kinos; there didn't seem to be much love in his makeup as far as women were concerned. They were merely there to be made use of whenever he felt the need.

And the accusation he had made to her? Holly's steps slowed as she pondered it. Okay, so she had met other men during the course of her work, and many of them had shown more than a passing interest, and a few had wanted to get serious, to establish a permanent relationship if she would let them. But she had always resisted this, giving Jamie and her work as her excuse. But in her heart she had always been afraid; afraid to give her trust and love to another man, unable to give herself completely in case they let her down. She knew she couldn't live through that hurt again. Better to go through life alone, without love, than that. And this was the main reason why she had never bothered to get a divorce; the fact that she was married could be used as an excuse to break off a relationship that was becoming too serious, gave her a loophole to escape through without too many recriminations. Her mouth twisted into a wry smile; did Nick, too, use his extinct marriage as a means of avoiding any entanglements with his women?

After a light lunch at the *taverna*, Holly spent the afternoon in her room, resting and working on the questions she would ask Felix Riddell, if she ever got to see him. The editor of the paper had been conducting delicate negotiations with an employee of Riddell's, who said he could get the millionaire to give an interview, but only if he—the employee— received a substantial fee in advance. Normally the newspaper wouldn't have touched such a dicey operation. There was too much chance of the man absconding with the money without their getting anything in return, but this would be such a scoop if they brought it off that the editor had decided to pursue it. Now they seemed on the point of agreement, having already paid a sum into a Swiss bank account as a sign of good faith, but Holly had a check in her purse for a whistle-making sum, which she was to give to the employee only after the interview if she could possibly manage it, but if he proved really insistent she was to pay him in advance if it was reasonably sure that the deal would go through. But at the moment she *didn't even know the man's name;* she only knew that he would get in touch with the newspaper and tell them where she could contact him, and also that he had insisted that a woman journalist be sent. Why, she didn't know, but could only guess that it was because Felix Riddell had specified it. Why he should specially ask for a woman Holly found rather intriguing; she had had to handle amorous celebrities who wanted to swap their story for sex before, and her editor had always made it clear that in such circumstances she was to chuck the story, but she had no serious qualms that this might be the reason with Felix Riddell. He had the power to order as many beautiful women as he wanted to his island and they would come running at his call.

She went to the window and looked out pensively at the dark shape of the island away on the horizon, wondering how long she would have to wait before she made contact. A movement on the quay caught her eye and she glanced down to see Nick strolling along to his boat, the sun on his face. Immediately she went to draw back, but before she could do so he looked up and saw her. His eyes held hers for a moment, and then he raised his hand in mocking salute before jumping onto his boat and going below.

Holly felt a sudden, fervent wish that this assignment would soon be over, that she could interview Felix Riddell and then go home just as fast as plane and boat could take her.

CHAPTER THREE

THE PHONE CALL Holly had been waiting for came at five o'clock that evening. The voice of the features editor was terse. "It's all set up, Holly. Our man got in touch with us through our Athens correspondent. We've told him where you're staying and he's going to contact you, probably tonight. So make sure you stay at the *taverna* and keep yourself available. And you must be alone, of course. Now," his tone became anxious, "you're sure you can handle this, Holly?"

"Yes, of course I am. Don't worry." She made soothing noises down the phone and had to listen all over again to a lot of instructions she'd already heard back in London.

"And you've done your homework? Learned all the trick questions to make sure it really is Riddell?"

Holly reassured him again and eventually he let her go, but not without misgivings, she knew; he would much rather have sent a seasoned male reporter on this job than a woman. She returned to her room bursting with excitement. So it was really on at last. She glanced at her watch, wondering when she would be contacted and where the interview would take place. On Felix Riddell's island of

Fallipos, she presumed, which could mean a short sea voyage. The breeze off the Mediterranean could be chilly at night, so she decided to change into something warmer and put on a pair of crisp white slacks and a navy sports shirt, with a chunky knitted jacket to put on if it got really cold. Then she checked that she had a new cassette and a couple of spares for the tape recorder, as well as her notebook and pens; she was going to make absolutely sure that she got every word of this interview. She packed these into her equipment bag, double-checked all her photographic gear and then, after some consideration, took a small, slim camera with a built-in flash from her equipment bag and slipped it into the pocket of her slacks, a critical look in the mirror reassuring her that its outline didn't show under her loose shirt, and if she carried her jacket on that side she would be doubly sure. Felix Riddell had allowed cameramen to take his photograph during his playboy years, but whether he would still do so now she would just have to wait and see.

Satisfied that she had made all the preparations she could, Holly picked up a paperback with which to while away the waiting time and went down to the terrace, and chose a table near the front, where she could see and be seen easily. It was early for dinner yet, so she ordered an ouzo and sipped it slowly, her nerves on edge and her eyes alert for anyone who looked at all out of place and who might be a likely contact.

For over an hour nothing happened, although in her nervous state nearly every man who walked along the harbor seemed shifty and suspicious, but

most of them were just fishermen going along to
their boats to prepare for the night's fishing. Several
men came to the *taverna*, but they were mostly in
twos or threes. Once she stiffened, her hopes rising,
as a lone man seemed to look straight at her and
then strode purposefully to the *taverna* and up the
steps. Her hand began to tremble a little as he came
toward her, but then he had gone past and joined a
group of men at a table behind her. Holly gave a little
gasp and then laughed at herself; it was probably too
early yet—there were too many people around.

Deciding to order dinner, she summoned the
waiter and with his help ordered *souvlaka*, which,
he assured her fervently, she would find most delicious. He picked up the menu and went to move
away, and Holly's heart skipped a beat as she realized a man was standing by her table, hidden from
her sight by the waiter. Then she saw that it was
Nick, and her heart skipped two beats.

"Hi. Mind if I join you?"

Before she could answer he had hooked out a
chair, throwing out an order to the waiter as he sat
down. Tonight he was wearing a lightweight blue
linen suit, the jacket cuffs turned back to reveal his
shirt sleeves, stark white against the strong brown-
ness of his hands. For a moment she was puzzled,
wondering why he was dressed so formally, then
she remembered the Frenchwoman's invitation to
drinks on her boat. So he'd succumbed to her
charms after all. A cold anger filled her; just like a
man, they could never resist even the most obvious
lures, even the most obnoxious of them thinking
themselves God's gift to women.

Then, almost as an afterthought, she came back to reality and remembered that she must be alone tonight. Forcefully she said, "Yes, I *do* mind."

"Sorry, what was that you said?" Nick, too, seemed to have been far away for a moment.

"I said that I do mind your sitting here. There are plenty of empty tables," she pointed out.

His eyes came up to study her face. "That's very unsociable of you."

"Very likely," she agreed coldly. "But nevertheless I'd prefer you to go and sit somewhere else."

The blue eyes, somehow made even bluer by the linen suit, narrowed speculatively. "Now I wonder why that is? It couldn't be because you've arranged to meet someone else, could it? And you've only been here a day—now that's what I call quick work," he added in mock admiration.

"No quicker than you and that tart who was chasing you all over the beach this morning," Holly retorted acidly.

A devilish look came into Nick's eyes as he raised his brows. "Surely you can't be referring to the luscious Chantel? Somehow I don't think she'd appreciate you referring to her as a tart. Quiche Chantel." He grinned in amusement.

"Well, you should know," Holly said crossly.

The grin broadened. "Do I detect a touch of jealousy in your voice?"

Holly glared at him. "No, you most certainly do not! She's as welcome to you as you obviously are to her. You should suit each other admirably," she added venomously.

The amused look left Nick's eyes and they

turned chill. "In some ways you haven't grown up at all, have you?"

Stifling a strong urge to tell him just how much she had grown up and why, Holly said coldly, "Look, just because we happen to have run into each other again doesn't mean that we have to be in one another's company all the time, does it? Personally I would have thought that we had quite enough of each other seven years ago to last a lifetime, otherwise we would never have parted." Steadily she added, "And I for one would have been quite happy *never* to have seen you again. So why don't you just take off and leave me to get along with my own life without unwelcome interruptions? I'm not interested in you, Nick, and I don't want you around."

"Well, you certainly made that clear enough." His face set into a tight mask, Nick stood up and gazed down at her for a moment, then turned abruptly and strode across to another table on the other side of the terrace, taking a chair facing into the café so that he could still see her clearly.

Holly looked down concentratedly at her book, trying to ignore him, wishing that he'd gone away instead of staying at the *taverna*. But inside she felt fiercely glad that she'd rebuffed him. It would have to have been said eventually, anyway; there was no way they could have kept running into one another, even casually, without all the old quarrels and anguish raising their heads again. It was better this way, to cut it off cleanly before too many hurtful words had been said. But nothing could prevent the memories—they were already there, bitter and bar-

ren, gnawing away at her confidence and composure.

The *souvlaka*, when it came, turned out to be
herb-flavored cubes of lamb threaded on a metal
skewer and grilled over charcoal. Served on a bed of
savory rice, it would indeed have tasted delicious if
Holly had had any appetite for it, but that had disappeared somehow, probably due to nervous tension
about the coming interview, and she only managed
less than half of the dish, much to the waiter's disappointment, who took it almost as a personal af-
front. Holly tried to reassure him, but she ended up
with a dessert she didn't really want, which the man
brought her as a gift from the proprietor who
thought she hadn't liked the *souvlaka*.

She rounded off the meal with coffee, all the
while acutely aware of Nick, who made no attempt
to hide the fact that he was watching her. He, too,
had a meal, which he took his time over, and afterward he didn't go away as she'd hoped, but, like
her, sat on over a drink, which meant that he
wasn't going to accept the Frenchwoman's invitation after all, she realized. It was well past nine already.

Lots more people came and went from the *taverna* as the night progressed, and Holly began to
get anxious; what if something had gone wrong and
her contact didn't come tonight. He might even
have seen her with Nick and hurriedly left, afraid
that he was being cheated. Holly sighed exasperatedly and ordered another coffee—better not to
have too much alcohol if she wanted to keep a clear
head for the interview. At ten the bouzouki music

started up again, coming from a speaker on the wall, first a tune of melancholy sadness, then changing tempo completely to one of gay abandon. After a while two or three men got up to dance the *syrtaki*, their arms linked, their legs bending and twisting energetically as they moved ever faster to the rhythm of the music.

Holly became so engrossed in watching the dancers that she forgot why she was there and turned with a start when someone gently touched her bare arm. Her expectations rose wildly, but it was only a small Greek boy of about ten, his long-lashed, smoky-brown eyes gazing up at her meltingly and in his hands a small tray with pieces of embroidered cloth and lace, probably made by his mother or sisters during the winter months.

"Please, miss, you buy?" He thrust the tray under her nose and looked at her expectantly.

Holly started to shake her head. "No, thanks, not right now."

But he pushed the tray nearer and said, "Yes, yes. You buy this one." He picked out an embroidered table mat folded in four and pushed it into her hands.

"Now look ...." Holly started to frown, then felt the crackle of paper inside the linen. Her heart suddenly beating very fast, she unfolded a corner of the cloth and lifted it so that she could see the piece of paper and quickly pulled it out so that she could read it. It contained only three words: "Follow the boy."

In a rather strangled voice she said, "Yes, I think I will buy it," and fished in her purse for some drachmas to put in the boy's outstretched hand. From the beautiful smile that lighted his face she had evidently given him far more than the mat was worth, but she was much too excited now to worry about being a corrupting influence on him. The boy moved away and went up to other tables where tourists were sitting, including Nick's, who merely waved him on, then the boy glanced back at Holly before turning to leave the *taverna*. As casually as she could, Holly finished her coffee, then pretended to yawn for the benefit of anyone who might be watching, particularly Nick, then picked up her bag and jacket and threaded her way to the steps. Nick watched her closely as she passed, but Holly kept her head turned away; let him think she was ignoring him if he liked; at the moment that suited her very well.

Her eyes had to adjust for a minute after leaving the bright lights of the *taverna*, but then she saw the boy's white shirt a few yards ahead of her to the left, heading for where the harbor ended and the town began. Quickly Holly fell in behind him, her rope-soled shoes making hardly any sound on the cobbles. The boy set quite a fast pace for his short legs and soon they were threading their way through the narrow twisting streets, until Holly began to feel hopelessly lost, and wondered uneasily where they were heading. Was the meeting to take place here in Melmia and not on Felix Riddell's island after all? It was impossible to catch up with the boy and ask him; every time she quickened her pace he, too, started to go faster until his thin legs were almost running, and even if she did manage to stop him he probably

wouldn't understand enough English to tell her
what she wanted to know. Once they stopped at a
white-painted house and she began to hope that
they'd reached their destination, but it must have
been the boy's house, for he went inside the lighted
doorway for only a moment and then came out mi-
nus the tray and started off again.

After another ten minutes they seemed to be
leaving the town, the houses thinning out and giving way to shabby fields where crickets sounded in
the coarse grass. Here and there appeared the
darker outline of several windmills, their eight trian-
gular-shaped sails still now, sleeping and waiting for
the dawn breeze. The boy left the paved road and
turned to the right into a farm track, the churned
mud of winter made by the passage of tractor and
lorry hardened now into deep ruts baked by the
sun. Grimly thankful that she had had the sense to
put on flat shoes, Holly stumbled on after the boy,
trying to find a flat path between the ruts, but she
wasn't used to this kind of rough exercise and was
soon out of breath and wondering just how much
farther they were going.

The track ran along beside a stone wall behind
which lay fields where sheep slept under the out-
spread branches of gnarled olive trees. It went on
for over half a mile before the stone wall came to an
abrupt end and the surface of the track changed,
became less rutted, and the hard earth gave way to
looser shingle underfoot.

At last the boy stopped and waited for Holly to
catch up with him. She took her heavy bag off her
shoulder and stood panting heavily, feeling her

shirt sticking to her and beads of moisture on her forehead.

"You wait here," the boy instructed in a hoarse whisper, his eyes bright in the pale light of the quarter moon, and Holly realized suddenly that the child was thoroughly enjoying himself. She grinned to herself, remembering that Jamie was into cowboys and Indians at the moment, and wondering what was the boy's equivalent—Greeks and Trojans, perhaps?

He went on alone and Holly stood looking around her while she recovered her breath. She could see now that they had traveled in a wide semicircle and were back on the coast, but higher up with quite a steep slope down to the sea that patterned first light and then dark, like molten silver, as the waves moved beneath the rays of the moon. To her right she could see a rocky headland jutting out into the sea and realized that it must be the left-hand arm of Melmia Bay. They had crossed behind it and come out into the bay beyond, a bay where the steep slope made building impractical and where there was no river to create a valley and give good grazing land. There was an outcrop of rock nearby and Holly moved over to sit on it, wondering how long she would have to wait and what would be at the end of it.

Then she heard a slight noise, the soft crunch of gravel underfoot, but it came, not from where the boy had gone toward the sea, but from behind her up the track that had led them here. Puzzled and more than a little nervous, she realized suddenly that she had a check for a very large sum of money in her bag, and that this was a very lonely place where a body could be easily dumped in the sea and disposed of. And no one knew she was there except the boy, and he was obviously very poor and could be paid to keep his mouth shut.

Her voice a tight, strangled sound close to terror, she said sharply, "Who is it? Who's there?"

The dark figure of a man, big and powerful, emerged from the shadow of a spreading tree and loomed toward her.

Holly opened her mouth to scream and then stared blankly with her mouth open. "You?" she gasped.

Nick emerged into the moonlight and said sharply, "Who did you expect?"

For a bewildering moment she thought that he was the man she had come to find, then reason returned as she realized that he must have followed her from the *taverna*. "What the hell are you doing here?" she demanded.

"I might ask you the same question. Rather an odd place to come for an evening stroll, isn't it? *And* with rather a strange companion. Why, Holly? Who have you come to meet?"

"How dare you follow me?" Her anger rose as she said furiously, "And just what right do you think you've got to pry into my business?"

"I still happen to be your husband—just in case it slipped your mind," he returned sarcastically.

"No," Holly returned angrily. "It hadn't slipped my mind. How could it when the sight of you brings it all back—all the whole, rotten, six months of it!"

Nick was beside her in two strides, his hand gripping her arm, his face murderous. "Why, you little bitch. If I'd had any sense I would have given you the hiding you deserved when we were together."

"Oh, really! That sort of line went out with the dinosaurs," Holly retorted disgustedly.

The grip on her arm tightened for a moment, then relaxed. "Maybe it did at that," Nick agreed. "And I doubt if even a hiding would have got through your total preoccupation with the social whirl you were caught up in at the time." He let her go and moved away a few paces. "But I still want to know who you came here to meet."

"I've already told you it's none of your business."

"Isn't it? You were scared to death when I came up behind you."

"Of course I was startled. I wasn't expecting anyone to come from that direction. And you'd be enough to frighten anyone, looming up out of the dark like that," she added nastily.

Nick laughed thinly. "We are getting down to basics tonight." He waited, but when she didn't speak, went on, "It's something to do with this newspaper assignment you're on, isn't it?"

"What if it is? How many times do I have to tell you it has nothing to do with you?"

"Maybe not. But I'm still going to hang around to make sure you're okay."

"But you can't!" Holly gazed at him in consternation. "You'll ruin everything. They stipulated that I come alone!" Realizing that last admission would have an adverse effect, she said hurriedly, in as reasonable a voice as she could manage. "Look, Nick, I—I appreciate your concern—" he snorted in disbelief but she ignored it and went on "—but I'm quite all right, really I am. I'm just waiting for some transportation to take me to an interview with someone—someone very important. I know following the boy here like this seems a bit way out, but he insisted on complete secrecy. And if you're seen with me, well, it could ruin the whole thing."

"Who is it?" he demanded bluntly.

"I can't tell you."

"Then I'll just stick around and find out."

"No!" Holly bit her lip, recognizing the look of implacable determination on his face. Desperately she tried another tack. "Look, I'm quite safe; they know who I am, but if they found you here they might turn nasty."

Nick gave a gasping laugh of disbelief. "Good God, do you think I'm afraid?"

Holly looked at the powerful set of his shoulders and for the first time began to wonder what had happened to him in those seven years, what had changed him into the man he had become. She turned her head away. "No, I'm sorry." Then, after a moment she went on, "This story means a lot to me, Nick. If I get it, it will be the most sensational thing I've ever pulled off. My success, or failure, could make it a real turning point in my career."

"And is your career that important to you?"

"Of course it is," she returned sharply. "It's my livelihood."

"Really?" he questioned disparagingly. "Or is it

just a way of passing the time between social engagements?''

"Oh, for God's sake don't be so damn patronizing! Do you still think that women only have marshmallow between the ears? I work because I have to,'' she told him, bitterness mingled with her fury.

From below them, carried on the still night, came the distinct sound of a boat grating on the shore, the sound of voices, talking low.

Holly gazed at him in despair. "Please Nick,'' she pleaded, she, too, lowering her voice to an urgent whisper.

He came closer, looking down at her intently. "I have to know who it is.''

She capitulated suddenly, knowing that she couldn't win. "His name is Felix Riddell. He lives on Fallipos, the island in the bay. *Now, will you please go?*''

But still he didn't move. "How long will you be there?''

"I don't know. It could be several hours. I just don't know how long it will take.''

Behind them they could hear the rattle of small stones as someone climbed up the slope.

Holly opened her mouth to make a last desperate plea but Nick forestalled her. "All right, I'm going. But I'll keep under cover and watch you safely on the boat.'' His hand came up to grip her elbow for a moment. "I just hope to hell that you know what you're doing.'' And then he melted into the dark shade of the trees while Holly turned thankfully to meet her contact.

The boy came first and then a man of medium

height but very thin build, his skin drawn so tightly onto his bones that when he turned to stare at Holly his face seemed almost cadaverous in the moonlight. He looked her over searchingly, then turned to slowly let his eyes travel all round, searching the darkness. Holly felt her heart thumping loudly and prayed that Nick was well hidden. The eyes in the gaunt face came back to her.

"You are alone?" the man asked in excellent English.

Holly nodded, not trusting herself to speak.

The man turned to the boy and gave him some money, at the same time issuing a curt order in Greek, so that the boy quickly took the money and ran off, back down the track toward the town.

Holly waited uneasily as the man eyed her again. "You have the money?"

"Yes."

"Give it to me," he commanded sharply.

Gripping her bag tighter, she said firmly, "Not until I'm quite sure I'm going to meet Felix Riddell. Where is he?"

The man's face tightened in anger, making his head more skull-like than ever. "I have already gone into all this with your paper. They know that they must trust me."

"They do—or I wouldn't be here," Holly said placatingly. "But surely at this stage you can tell me where he is, where the meeting is to take place?"

He paused, then shrugged. "Very well." He raised his arm to point out to sea. "He is on his yacht, the *Alexis*. I have a dinghy down on the beach and will row you out to him."

"He has agreed to this interview?" Holly asked, still suspicious.

"Yes, he has agreed," the man answered, almost too quickly.

"Then why like this, at night and in such secrecy, and on his yacht? Why not openly in daylight and at his house on the island? And just who are you and how do you fit into all this?" she demanded.

For a moment he glared at her, frowning, then seemed to make up his mind. "My name does not matter, but you can call me Stavros, if you wish. It is sufficient that you know I am close to Mr. Riddell. I was going to tell you everything on the way to the yacht, but if you insist I will tell you now. Some years ago Mr. Riddell was seriously ill, so ill that he almost died, but it affected his brain. And now—" he shook his head as if in sorrow "—now he hides away here so that no one can see what he has become."

Coming closer to her, he leaned forward and lowered his voice. "Some days he is completely normal, others he behaves like a child, but always he has his deformity to remind him."

Holly stared at him. "Deformity?"

"His face," the man explained. "It, too, was affected, and now he is hideous to look upon, grotesque. That is why he allows no one to come here. Even before his servants he must wear a mask."

Her eyes widening in appalled horror, Holly stared at him speechlessly. No wonder Felix Riddell had shut himself away from everyone and everything he had ever known. To change almost overnight from a sought-after playboy to little short of a

monster—the shock must have been almost un-
bearable!

But the man who called himself Stavros was going on. "He depends now to a great extent on
drugs. And sometimes, when he has a bad bout of
depression he likes to talk about his past, about his
feelings now and of the little future he has left to
him, but for some reason he will only talk to a
woman. But there are no women on the island; he
cannot bear to have one there in case they ever see
him without his mask, also because he is afraid they
will pity him. He is not, even now, a man who can
tolerate pity."

"So what women does he talk to, then?" Holly
asked, absolutely fascinated now by the man's
story.

"It does not happen often, you understand, but
several times now I have brought the boat here and
paid a woman to go out to his yacht." He must have
felt Holly stiffen beside him, because he added
hastily, "Please do not misunderstand me; he does
not touch these women. Such things are beyond
him now, but he likes to look at them and just talk
to them. They do not understand him, of course—
he speaks only in English, but that does not matter.
He is content that there is a woman there to listen
to his ramblings."

"Ramblings?"

"Yes, because no one asks him questions or
keeps him to the point."

"And you think I could do so?"

"If you know your job, yes. But you must be
gentle with him, not push him where he doesn't

want to go. He is very ill. I do not think he will live much longer."

Holly thought it over quickly; it all seemed feasible enough, but one thing still bothered her. "You still haven't told me how you come into this?" she reminded him.

Stavros shrugged eloquently. "I am a poor man. When Felix Riddell dies it will be hard for me to find work. I have read about the great sums that newspapers pay for stories so I thought of this. It can do him no harm—he no longer reads the papers—and perhaps it will do him some good. Maybe one of his ex-wives will read it and insist on visiting him. Give him some company in his last days."

"They might at that," Holly agreed, but wondered cynically whether it would be compassion that drew them or just to make sure that they were included in the millionaire's will. Then she chided herself for being overcynical; that was what working on a newspaper did to you—you saw too much of man's greed and ruthlessness.

But Stavros was speaking again. "You are satisfied now, Miss Weston?" An edge of sarcasm in his voice.

Holly nodded. "Yes. Take me out to the yacht, and I'll give you the money there."

"Come then."

He turned to lead the way down to the beach, the moon bright enough now for there to be no need of a torch. Holly took a quick look toward the clump of trees where Nick had been hiding, but he didn't show himself. She wondered uneasily how much he had heard and whether he would make use of the information; phone it through to a rival paper and steel her thunder, perhaps. Then she chided herself again; Nick might be the man she most loved to hate, but that was no reason to believe he might play such a dirty trick on her. Unless, of course, he equally hated her!

The path was steep and the shingle loose underfoot, but it seemed well trodden, and Holly wondered what it was used for, in such a quiet place out of sight of the harbor. A spot of smuggling, perhaps? A dinghy was drawn up half out of the water and Stavros helped her in and then pushed the boat out and jumped in after her and picked up the oars, sending the boat through the water with surprising ease for such a thin person.

"What have you got in there?" he asked, nodding toward her bag.

"Oh, it's just my tape recorder and photographic equipment."

His voice was suddenly sharp. "There must be no photographs. They are forbidden. Do you understand?"

"But if he's wearing his mask what difference can it make?" Holly protested.

"The flash could frighten him, make him realize what was happening. And then he could turn nasty and might hurt you before I could restrain him."

She looked at Stavros silently for a moment. Then she asked, "Are you some sort of nurse?"

"Yes." He looked over his shoulder to check on their heading. "Do you agree not to take any photographs, or shall I take you back to the shore?"

"Very well."

He continued rowing until they were well out to
sea, and then Holly saw the outline of a large yacht,
its only illumination an anchor light high on the
masthead. Stavros pulled round to the starboard
side and made the dinghy fast to some steps that
had been lowered from the side. He climbed out of
the boat and bent to help her up, then preceded her
up the stairs onto the deck. As soon as they reached
it he turned to her. "The money," he demanded,
holding out his hand.

Silently Holly took the check from her pocket
and handed it to him. He lifted it so that he could
see, then nodded, satisfied.

"This way."

He led her along a wooden deck, so highly polished that it reflected the moonlight, to a sun
lounge and on through double doors leading to an
inner cabin. It was too dark to see much, but Holly
got the impression of luxury from the thickness of
the carpet under her feet and the gleam of silvered
mirrors and onyx tables. The place literally smelled
expensive. There was a glow of light in the inner
cabin, low down, near the floor, and she realized
with a shock that it came from an open fire built
into the bulkhead, the almost dead coals giving an
unpleasant warmth to the darkened room.

But it was the man who sat in an antique straight-
backed wing chair near the fireplace who held all
Holly's attention. He sat in the chair, gripping the
arms, looking straight ahead at the curtained window, although there was nothing to see, and on his
head he wore a black hood, like a close-fitting bala-

clava, with holes for his eyes and slits for his nose and mouth. Holly thought that it was the most terrible thing she had ever seen.

Stavros moved quietly over to the chair and said softly, "Mr. Riddell? Mr. Riddell, are you asleep?"

The man started. "No. No, I'm not asleep. What do you want?"

His speech was slow and slurred, almost as if he was drunk.

"I have brought someone to talk to you. A nice young lady. See, here she is."

He beckoned Holly forward into the dim light of the fire. The man who had once been the most sought-after jet-setter in the world lifted his head in pathetic eagerness.

"You will sit with me?"

Holly nodded dumbly.

Stavros moved a chair forward for her, but even before he'd done so Felix Riddell started to talk, and Holly hastily reached into her bag, took out her cassette player, and set it onto Record. For good measure she took out her pad and pencils, but it was difficult to see in the flickering light and he was going very fast, but rambling as Stavros had said, describing a big party he'd given in Monte Carlo one year. As soon as she'd taken her things out, Stavros picked up her bag and moved it out of the way, making sure she couldn't take any photographs.

Breaking in on his outpourings, she said gently, "Did you like giving parties, Mr. Riddell?"

He seemed startled that she had spoken back at first and was slow in answering, but at length said mumblingly, "Yes, yes. Always liked parties."

"Even when you were a child? When you lived in Toronto?" Holly asked, putting in the first of her catch questions.

"Yes, always liked parties," he repeated. Then, after a moment he added, "But didn't live in Toronto. Lived in Quebec."

Behind her she heard Stavros give a hiss of warning and decided she'd better be less obvious next time. She led him on to give her his life story, and as he told her about some of the business methods he had used and the names of some of the women he'd had affairs with, Holly began to get increasingly excited. This was really hot stuff! Her second catch question, about one of his wives, he got right immediately and even put her right on a mistake she'd made in all innocence, so that she was convinced that he was indeed Felix Riddell. Still, it wouldn't hurt to throw in one more to make absolutely sure.

Using a piece of information she'd culled from an obscure Canadian publication, she said, "And you were with your second wife and your stepchildren, Jodi and Paul, when you entertained the American president on your yacht, *The Dolphine*, weren't you?"

"That's right, not this yacht. *The Dolphine*. Gave that to my wife."

"And Mrs. McGraw came, too, didn't she? The president brought her?"

The voice wavered. "Yes, he brought her. Very beautiful woman. Very good friend of the president's."

Holly let him go on talking, but sat stiffly now, her ears pricked to catch every word. Mrs. McGraw had been a she, all right—and a bitch at that—but she was the president's dog! It was only a small thing, of course, and he might genuinely not have remembered, but it was enough to make her wary and by listening attentively she later caught him in another slip when he got the name of one of his companies wrong, a lesser one, admittedly, but one that he first started with and had always owned, so you would expect him not to have to think twice about the name. And he seemed to be telling her too many things that would be of great interest to a newspaper, sensational revelations, instead of the ordinary everyday things you would expect him to dwell on when he was so ill.

The fire had soon died right down, leaving the cabin in almost complete darkness, but it was very hot in there with all the windows shut and the curtains drawn, and Stavros had twice quietly brought drinks for them. She had been there for a long time now, already she had had to change the cassette in the recorder, and Felix Riddell's voice had slowed, become hoarser and he had often to reach for his drink. Holly listened and watched him as best she could in growing suspicion, but was careful to let none of it show in her voice, her mind busily trying to find a way of proving once and for all whether the man was really Felix Riddell. It was quite some time before she realized from the noise of his movements that he might be lifting his mask when he drank. Once he even took something from his pocket, a handkerchief, she supposed, to mop his face, which must have been absolutely boiling under the hood.

Slowly, still asking questions, Holly eased the minicamera from the pocket of her slacks and with a soft click opened it, ready to use. Lifting it to where she judged his face to be, she waited for Felix Riddell to take another drink. The cabin was very quiet, really; there was only the drone of his voice as he talked of a bribe he'd given to a high-up politician, and the low whine of the cassette recorder. The presence of Stavros, sitting silently in the background, she had almost forgotten, she was so wholly concentrating on waiting for the right moment.

It came at last. She heard him move forward and the chink of the glass, then a blur of darker movement as he lifted up his hand to raise the mask. The built-in flash exploded into light and revealed the man with the mask pulled well up off his face. He had swarthy features—a hooked nose, and a heavily jowled chin. An ugly face, admittedly, but not one that had been deformed and misshapen by disease, and bearing no resemblance to the dozens of photographs of the handsome playboy that Holly had studied before this assignment. So whoever the man was, he wasn't Felix Riddell!

After the blinding glare of the flash there was a shocked silence into which Holly said coolly, "You might as well turn the lights on Stavros. I've seen through your game even without them."

The lights snapped on, revealing the opulent luxury of the cabin; the red leather chesterfields, the blue-period Picasso on the wall set between ornate wall lights.

She turned to Stavros. "Nice try, but not quite good enough."

The man who had pretended to be Felix Riddell pulled the mask off his head and brought out a handkerchief to wipe a face dripping with sweat. "Where did we go wrong?" His voice now quite clear and normal.

Holly smiled thinly. "Does it matter?" She turned to Stavros. "I'll take back that check."

He had got to his feet and stood glaring at her, his face more like a death's head than ever. "I think not. After all, we deserve something for all the trouble we have gone to."

His voice was low, menacing, and Holly suddenly realized the danger of the position she was in. The other man, too, had got to his feet and stood looking at her, an ugly grin on his face.

"What a silly little girl you are," he said jeeringly. "Did you really think we'd tamely hand back that kind of money?"

Holly shrugged, trying to keep the fear out of her voice. "All right, but you obviously know a lot about Felix Riddell, so why don't you tell me the true story?" Bending down, she picked up the cassette player off the table and pretended to rewind it.

Stavros laughed gratingly. "If we'd had a story to sell we would have sold it long ago. A trick like this was our last resort."

"And I suppose you hoped that I'd just hand the money over so that you wouldn't have to go through this charade?" Holly said as evenly as she could, her eyes darting around the cabin for a means of escape.

"Oh, no, we knew we'd have to go through with it when your paper insisted on paying us by check, instead of in cash, as we wanted. We knew that we needed time to cash the check and get away." He laughed harshly. "So don't think we're going to let you get off the boat and stop the check, as you're hoping. You're not going anywhere for quite some time, if at all."

Holly pretended to take a few fearful paces away from him, bringing her near to the cabin wall—not that the fear was in any way a pretense! "You can't do that. You have no right to keep me here!"

They both began to move toward her from either side of the big cabin.

"Can't we?" Stavros said, a foul grin splitting his skeletonlike face. "I think we can do anything we like to you. In fact, it might be quite pleasantly interesting *having* you here."

Putting everything she had into it, Holly suddenly looked past them at the door and shrieked, "Nick, help!"

In the instant that they both automatically turned toward the door, she threw the casette recorder across the cabin at the far light fixture and at the same time reached up to the wall light above her head, catching at the ornate brass arm and pulling it with all her strength. There was the rending sound of metal tearing away from the wood paneling as the screws holding the fitting came away from their sockets, and then the electrical wires started to appear and got stuck. The far light bulb had exploded into tiny particles of flying glass when the cassette player hit it and the men had instinctively ducked, but now they saw what was happening and came charging toward her. Holly gave one last, desperate pull and the wires came free again. Then, mercifully, there was a loud bang as the system fused and the cabin was once again plunged into darkness.

Holly took a wide leap to the side just in time, and behind her heard the two men curse as they collided into one another.

"The door! Quickly, cover the door!" one of them shouted.

But she had already thought of that and had decided to try to get out by one of the windows instead while the men knocked into each other in the darkness as they searched for her. Pushing aside the curtains, she spent several agonizing seconds feeling for a catch, then held her breath as she fumbled it open and quietly, hardly breathing, started to slide the window open.

"Quiet! What was that?" Stavros called out as the window squeaked a little.

"I heard nothing. Where the hell is she?" the other man returned furiously.

Holly picked up a low table near her and flung it across the cabin in the direction of where she thought the door was. The men gave a shout and started for the noise, and in those few precious seconds of confusion Holly was up and had scrambled unceremoniously through the window and had started to run along the deck away from the cabin. There was no moon now and it was too early for dawn—even the anchor light was out—she must have fused every light on the boat. Twice she stumbled into things in the darkness, banging her hip quite painfully so that she almost cried out, but she hobbled on looking for somewhere to hide where the men wouldn't find her, somewhere small where she could curl up and be safe. Of how she was to get off the boat she didn't even think. It would be impossible to try to steal the dinghy and row away—that was the first place they would expect her to go to. No, better to hide and wait for daylight. The boat couldn't sail on indefinitely. It would have to refuel sometime. Then she felt something hard and uneven underfoot, and stooping down found that it was a ring set into the deck, which meant that there must be a hatch underneath. If she could hide in there . . . .

She bent to pull it, but just then a torch shone into her face and Stavros shouted, "Got you!"

He made a grab for her that she evaded and then she started to run, but her foot caught in the deck ring she had pulled up, she was thrown off balance against the rail and then fell headlong over it, plunging down the length of the boat's side into the blackness of the sea.

She seemed to go down forever before at last she managed to turn and strike out for the surface, her clothes weighing her down and her stomach full of the water she had swallowed when her scream had suddenly been cut off as she had hit the sea. Treading water, she coughed and spluttered, despair in her heart because now the men would come for her and take her back to the boat. Looking up she saw Stavros shining the torch over the side and lifted a hand to him. The beam of light caught her and she heard the man laugh. He shouted something to the other man, but he made no move to come for her and then, unbelievably, she heard the boat's high-powered engines throb into life. My God, were they going to run her down?

Swiftly she turned and began to swim as fast as she could out of range of the torch, then veered off at a tangent in the hope that they would go the other way. She thought that if they did catch up with her she might be able to dive deep enough for the boat not to hit her, but it was the screws she was afraid of; on such a big boat they might be powerful enough to suck her into them and cut her to pieces.

Kicking off her shoes, she swam as she'd never swum before, but her slacks were dragging her down with every stroke and she had to waste a few vital minutes while she pulled them off and also her shirt, letting them sink to the bottom. She made much better progress then, and when she at last stopped to rest she saw that the boat was a good distance away, seemingly going around in ever widening circles, the torch playing on the water as the men searched for her in vain.

Pretty confident now that she had outdistanced them, Holly began to worry that the sea might do the men's job for them. All she knew was that she was somewhere in the Mediterranean and had no idea which way to turn to reach the nearest land—if there was any within swimming distance, that is. Then she took herself in hand to balk the rising panic; the boat had been anchored only a quarter of a mile or so from Kinos. If she kept going she must reach it soon. If she was heading in the right direction *and* if the current didn't carry her right past it, of course. But she couldn't just tread water and wait for daylight as she would very much like to have done. The men might come upon her, and the current would carry her along anyway, so she might just as well swim.

It was nearly three hours later before the gray cold light of dawn revealed the low dark mass of land only a few hundred yards away to her right. If the sun hadn't come up she would have gone on swimming right by it. Trembling with exhaustion and cold, Holly from somewhere found hidden reserves of strength and swam doggedly toward it. Her legs gave way as she reached the beach and she had to crawl out of the water on her hands and knees, collapsing, her last dregs of energy gone, as she reached the soft cool sand.

The sun had dried her and was burning hot on Holly's back before she opened her eyes again. Someone was stooping over her and she looked up to see a familiar face examining her.

"Well, well. A mermaid, no less. Welcome to my island, Miranda," the real Felix Riddell said with a smile on his still extremely handsome face.

CHAPTER FOUR

HOLLY STARED AT FELIX RIDDELL bemusedly, her mind refusing to believe what her eyes told her. He reached down and helped her to her feet, but she was still so weak that she had to cling to his arm for support.

"Where...where did you say this was?" she asked unsteadily.

"Fallipos. Didn't you know?"

"No. No, I thought I was swimming the other way, to Kinos."

"And you missed your way—how unfortunate."

There was irony in Felix Riddell's voice, but it was lost on Holly. She remembered the way the yacht had come after her and her long, despairing swim and she began to shake uncontrollably, her teeth chattering despite the heat of the day.

"Here, you'd better have this." He let go of her for a moment while he slipped off his open-fronted shirt and then helped her to put it on. It was only then that Holly realized that her bra must have come off when she was swimming, and she hastily raised her hands to cover herself.

"Oh, it's much too late for that. I've already seen *all* your charms." His eyes wandered down her body and settled.

Holly glanced down, too, and saw that where her nylon panties were still wet at the front they were quite transparent. She flushed and hurriedly turned away from him.

"If . . . if you'll be kind enough to lend me a towel and some dry clothes I'd be very grateful, Mr. Riddell," she said stiffly, his tone getting through to her.

"You know who I am, then?"

"Yes," she admitted.

"And I suppose that after I've given you some clothes you'd like to stay and talk to me for a'while, is that it?"

Holly would have liked just that very much, but she could tell from his manner that it was the last thing that was likely to happen. She turned her head to look at him.

"I . . . I don't know what you mean?"

"Don't you? Oh, I think you do. You're not the first reporter who's tried this means of getting an interview with me, you know. But I must admit that you're the most attractive yet. Although the last woman was Italian and was completely naked," he added mendaciously.

Holly pulled the shirt tighter around her and began to walk back along the beach. Felix Riddell followed her a few paces behind.

"Is there somewhere I can hire a boat to take me back to Kinos?"

"It can be arranged. And you won't have to pay, it will be my pleasure to provide it. Besides, I hardly think you were able to carry any money about your, er, person." Holly's back stiffened but she kept on walking silently. After a few moments he said sarcastically, "You're not trying to tell me by this air of injured dignity that you're not a reporter, are you?"

Holly stopped and turned to face him. "No, I'm not a reporter. I'm a photojournalist."

For a moment amusement shone in his eyes as he came up to her. "Oh, that's quite another thing, of course." Then the eyes grew steely. "But leading to the same thing. You used this trick to come here and interview me, didn't you? Tried to use my well-known susceptibility to female charms to reach me? And how far were you prepared to go, I wonder? The Italian woman assured me that I could do anything I wanted."

Holly had been through a lot since last night, and this sort of sexual crudity was the last straw. Close to tears she yelled at him angrily, "Damn you, Felix Riddell! Yes, I did come to Greece to interview you. But only because it had already been fixed up between my paper and one of your employees. And then last night, when I got on your yacht, I found they'd cheated me. It was only a man pretending to be you, after all." Her voice broke on something dangerously close to a sob. "And when I found out, they tried to keep me on the boat, but I ran away and fell overboard. And then they tried to run me down, and I've been swimming and swimming for hours. And now you start being damned rude, and it's just about the last straw! So if you'll tell me where I can get a boat, I'll leave you and your rotten island just as soon as I can!" Then, like a fool, she burst into tears and had to turn and run away from him up the beach to hide her face.

He let her go and waited for a good five minutes before coming up to where she was sitting on a stone seat at the beginning of a flight of broad, shallow steps leading up from the beach. Holly wiped the back of her hand across her eyes and blinked up at him. His body, in just a pair of blue Bermuda shorts, was still fit and athletic even though he must have been nearing fifty. Whatever he did on his island, he hadn't let himself go to seed.

Sitting down beside her, he said, "It seems there is more to this than I thought. What's your name?"

"Holly Weston."

He glanced down at her ringless fingers. "Well, Miss Holly Weston, you'd better tell me exactly how you got here."

Holly would very much like to have showered the sea salt from her body and hair and to have borrowed some fresh clothes before she did so, but she realized that she probably wouldn't ever get these out of Felix Riddell unless she told her story first. He seemed quite ruthless enough to just put her in a boat and send her back to Kinos as she was. So, haltingly at first, she told him the whole story, everything.

"I realize I was an utter fool to believe Stavros," she admitted finally, "but it seemed so plausible—you being struck down by some illness and losing your looks. Why else would you imprison yourself here?"

He looked at her enigmatically. "Why, indeed?" Standing up, he pulled her to her feet. "You'd better come up to the house, and I'll find you some clothes."

She looked at him uncertainly. "You do believe me, don't you?"

"These men—what did they look like?"

"The one who pretended to be you was dark and swarthy, and the other one, Stavros—" she shuddered "—was awful, terribly thin with a face like a skull, as if it had no flesh on it."

Riddell had stopped and was staring at her intently. A look of fierce anger grew in his eyes as he said, "*Now* I believe you. The swarthy one—he was my valet for several years until I had to dismiss him recently. And the other is the chief mechanic on my yacht. At the moment he is supposed to have it out for sea trials after some repairs. They must have plotted this together and waited until they had an excuse to take the yacht before they sent word to you. Yes, yes, they could have done it. I gave the captain and the rest of the crew leave this week. What exactly did they tell you?" he demanded abruptly.

As Holly told him they walked together up the steps and emerged into a garden, a green paradise where no such trees or flowers should ever have grown. It could only have been created by transporting tons of earth to cover the barren rocks. The plants, from exotic flamboyant trees of the West Indies to English roses, tenderly grown and constantly watered, made a haven of shade with here and there a lawn and sheltered bowers heavily fragrant with hanging honeysuckle or bougainvillea. They came to a little white stone circular temple, its domed roof supported by statues of ancient Greek goddesses that looked as old as those she'd seen at the Temple of Diana at Ephesus, and just as beautifully sculptured. But she was given no time to stand and stare, for Felix Riddell strode briskly along another, wider path set between a bank of hibiscus bushes, their large scarlet flowers glowing in the sun, and then up another flight of steps that wound up a quite steep hillside and out onto the terrace of his villa. And now Holly just had to stop and stare— the villa was built into the hillside, and its rooms with their stone balconies and the outside twisting staircases, half hidden by exotic trailing plants, all seemed to be a part of the rock slope. There was even a waterfall that cascaded down to a swimming pool set into a paved patio.

"But...but it's beautiful," Holly breathed. "Is the waterfall for real?"

The millionaire shook his head. "No, it's pumped down from a tank on top of the hill." He went to hurry on, but turned back when Holly laughed.

She looked at him in amusement. "How unromantic. You really should at least have said that it came from a stream that has magic powers; and that the ancient gods and goddesses drank from it—that would have been even better, of course." Then she shrugged. "But I don't suppose you'd bother with all that for someone who's just an unwanted intruder."

Felix Riddell studied her face, almost as if he was seeing it for the first time, his eyes going over her fair hair, still speckled with sand, the gray eyes beneath fine level brows, her straight nose and the clean lines of her mouth and chin. Holly tilted her head rather defiantly under his regard, and he said abruptly, "How old are you?"

She frowned but saw no reason for not telling him. "I'm twenty-four."

He shook his head almost in disbelief. "And I suppose you're hopelessly romantic?"

Holly looked away and reached out to touch a trailing stem of purple bougainvillea, concentrating on it. "I was once."

"But you're not anymore?"

"No."

"I see."

She turned her face to look at him. "Do you?"

"Oh, yes." He smiled wryly.

Remembering his past history, she said, "Yes, I suppose you do."

She let go of the spray of flowers and by tacit consent they both turned and walked silently toward the villa.

He led the way through wide patio doors that stood open to the sun and into a large room that was a surprise; Holly had expected to see sumptuous decor and priceless ornate, antique furniture, but the room was really very plain, with a polished wooden floor with just two or three brightly colored locally woven rugs, and rough-cast walls painted white to give a stark background to several French impressionist paintings that even to Holly's untrained eyes spelled Van Gogh and Utrillo. The furniture, too, was plain; a couple of settees with deep, squashy cushions, a baby grand piano in one corner, and the only concession to conventional ideas of luxury was a really good set of stereo equipment and a whole wall of shelves filled with records and tapes.

"You'd better come through to my communications center first, and then I'll find you some clothes."

Riddell led the way up a spiral staircase and into a corridor with several rooms opening off it, the doors all tantalizingly shut. The communications center made Holly's eyes pop. It was almost like walking into an airplane cockpit, with a huge and complicated-looking radio transmitter, telex machines that clattered continuously, racks of telephones in different colors, as well as several computer systems. There were two men manning the room, and Felix Riddell crossed to speak to one of them, who immediately picked up a phone and began to talk into it urgently.

"We should have a trace of the yacht within an hour," the millionaire said as he rejoined her. "Although if they think that you were drowned, they might even bring it back of their own account, thinking themselves safe." He smiled grimly. "It will be interesting to see their faces when they find you here waiting for them."

Holly, too, found that thought very satisfying after the way they'd tried to run her down. Then she realized that the first thing they would do, whether the men returned to Fallipos or not, would be to cash the check she'd paid them. Catching his arm as he was turning to go out of the room, she said quickly, "Mr. Riddell, may I ask you a favor? The check I gave to Stavros—could you please telex my newspaper and ask them to stop payment on it immediately?"

His eyebrows rose and he said rather scathingly, "They got the money out of you, did they?"

Her voice hardening, Holly retorted, "I thought they'd delivered the goods!"

He laughed, suddenly seeming ten years youn-
ger. "A drugged and masked caricature of me being
the goods?"

Holly decided to get her own back a little. "Well,
he did seem to know an awful lot about your past
life. Especially about your women—he knew a great
deal of detail about those."

His eyes narrowed. "Did he, by God." Then he
added, blandly, "I hope you didn't believe it. Anyone who could make up such a plausible reason for
my being here would obviously make up those
sorts of sordid details, as well—just to titillate you
and make you forget the more important things
he'd glossed over, of course."

Holly's mouth opened as she realized that he was
mocking her, but before she could make a retort he
turned and said, "Come along, I'll show you where
you can change."

He went down another corridor that opened into
a gallery overlooking a huge dining room that had a
great fireplace stacked with logs in one corner—a
luxurious extravagance on an island where every
log would have to be shipped in from the mainland.
He halted by a door farther along the gallery and
said, "You'll find everything you want in here.
When you've finished go down the outside stairs to
the patio." Then he pushed open the door, gave
her a brief nod and walked briskly back toward the
communications center.

This room had yielded to modern comforts more
than the others Holly had seen, with a wooden
four-poster bed hung with flowered chintz, a dressing table, and soft carpet underfoot. It was one of

the rooms with a balcony overlooking the garden, and Holly immediately went to stand on it and look out at this green paradise set in the clearest of seas and under the bluest of skies. For a few minutes she just drank in the beauty of the place: the richness of the flower-filled garden, the warmth of the sun, the heavy scent of the oleander that draped its red flowers like colorful curtains on either side of the balcony, and the silence broken only by the soft murmur of the sea and the gentle buzz of a honeybee that drank its fill from the silken flower heads. Perhaps for the first time in her life she began to realize just what money could do and how it could enhance the lives of those who possessed it in unlimited quantities. That it could create something as perfectly beautiful as this she had never imagined in her wildest dreams.

Turning back into the room she discovered a bathroom opening off it and also a dressing room lined with wardrobes that, when she opened the doors, she found to be full of women's clothes, all new from the looks of them and bearing labels that made her stare reverently. And there weren't only clothes, but also dozens of pairs of shoes in several sizes and drawers full of delicate lace underwear, all still in their packaging. Holly gazed in awe, wondering just who all the things were intended for; hardly for chance visitors like herself, so presumably Felix Riddell still had female guests on the island from time to time, and far more than just one if the variety of sizes and colors was anything to go by.

Holly took her time over her shower, using the shower lotion she found in the bathroom together

with an expensive shampoo for her hair. Then she
wrapped herself in a thick bath towel not much
smaller than a bed sheet and padded back into the
bedroom where she explored the dressing-table
drawers until she found a hair dryer; by now she
was quite sure that Felix Riddell had overlooked
nothing that would add to the comfort of his female
guests. She spent a blissful half hour looking
through the clothes and would dearly have loved to
try most of them on, but in the end she chose the
simplest sundress and sandals that she could find,
feeling that as she was only an uninvited and unwelcome intruder she had no right to anything at all, let
alone something expensive. But she did go a little
overboard with the Joy perfume she discovered,
together with a large makeup kit in one of the
drawers, but then what woman could possibly resist
the scent advertised as the most expensive perfume
in the world?

Almost reluctantly, she left the lovely room and
walked along the balcony to where the outside staircase was cut into the rock face, twisting down to be
for a while in deep shadow and then in bright sunlight where jasmine flowers cascaded over the bal-
ustrade and shafts of the sun's rays turned the
stone to gold, a metamorphic change surpassing
that of any ancient alchemist.

Felix Riddell was waiting for her on the patio,
seated at a round garden table and with another casual shirt over his shorts. He looked up as she ap-
proached and quite openly studied her as she
walked toward him, his eyes running over her ap-

praisingly. But he made no comment on her appearance, merely motioning her to a chair.

"I expect you're hungry?"

"Mmm, starving."

"Then I'll order breakfast for you. You'll have to excuse me not joining you, but I had mine some time ago."

"Of course. What is the time?" Holly asked. "Unfortunately my watch wasn't waterproof and it's stopped. And I didn't see a clock anywhere."

"You won't," Riddell answered with a short laugh. "That was one of the first things I did away with when I came here. No more living by the clock and chasing time, cramming as much into the day as I possibly could. The only place where there's a clock now is in the communications center where I have a digital international time clock so that I don't get people out of bed when I telephone them. No, here on Fallipos I let time take its course, with the result that it almost seems to stand still. But, if you really want to know what the time is—" he glanced up at the angle of the sun "—then I'd say it was between ten-thirty and eleven o'clock."

Holly had been smiling to herself while he'd been speaking and now he turned his head and caught her. "I suppose you think that's a very Bohemian attitude to life?" he demanded rather sneeringly.

Holly laughed. "No, I think it's a wonderful attitude if one is rich enough in money—or time—to do it. No, I was just wondering what all the sales staff of the quartz-watch manufacturing company you own would say if they could hear you."

He grinned. "I guess it wouldn't be very good for business, would it?"

An elderly servant came then with a heavily laden breakfast tray, and Holly bit hungrily into the hot rolls spread with homemade butter and honey, washed down with several cups of American coffee. While she ate, her host asked her questions about her career and these she answered readily enough, telling him about some of her previous assignments and her early years in journalism.

"You're rather young to be sent on a job like this, aren't you?"

"I suppose so," Holly confessed, "but there aren't that many female photojournalists around, especially those who can take off at a moment's notice to more or less anywhere in the world."

"You intended to take photographs of me?"

"I hoped to." She smiled ruefully. "But I had to abandon all my gear on board your yacht, and I expect Stavros will have thrown it overboard by now so there won't be any evidence that I was ever aboard. Lord, my editor will go mad when he hears he has to replace that little lot." A thoughtful smile curved her mouth. "I wonder how Stavros will explain the light fixture I broke. Perhaps he's pulled into some port now and is desperately trying to get it fixed before he brings the yacht back." Then she looked at him rather guiltily. "I'm sorry about the lights, but it was rather an emergency, you understand?"

"Oh, quite," he answered gravely. "Please feel free to pull my boat to pieces anytime you like."

Holly looked at him quickly, saw the amusement

in his eyes and laughed. Sitting back in her chair, she said with a sigh, "Oh, it is good to be alive."

His eyes became grave again. "It was very foolish of you to go off with them without some sort of safeguard. Didn't you tell them at the hotel where you were going?"

Holly shook her head. "I wasn't sure exactly where I was going myself. And you have to be prepared to take risks if you want to get good stories."

"Where are you staying? I'll get someone to call and let them know you're safe."

"Oh, that won't be necessary, thanks. I'm only staying at a *taverna* in Melmia, and I'm sure no one there will worry about me if ...." She stopped suddenly remembering Nick and went on slowly, "...if I stay out all night."

But Felix Riddell had seen her hesitation and picked it up quickly. "There is someone?"

She shook her head. "I remembered that I did tell someone that I was going to interview you, but I'm sure he won't have given it another thought."

"He?"

"An Englishman I know who happens to be on holiday here."

Thankfully a buzzer sounded discreetly then, preventing him from questioning her further as he picked up the receiver of a telephone and listened for several minutes. Then he replaced it and smiled with some satisfaction. "My yacht has been traced to Piraeus, the seaport that serves Athens, and I have arranged for the two men to be brought back here."

"The police will bring them?"

"No, not the police. I have my own means of dealing with those who are disloyal to me."

Holly looked at him and shivered suddenly, glimpsing for a moment the cold ruthlessness that had carried him to the heights of power and fortune. Not for anything would she want to be in the shoes of Stavros and the other man when they faced Felix Riddell.

He gave her his attention again, saying, "You say that you can take off at a moment's notice; does that mean that you have no family commitments?"

"Well, I do," Holly answered carefully, "but I have them organized so that I'm able to do my job."

"I see. And just what are your commitments? Parents, boyfriends? A lover, perhaps?"

Holly's features tightened at the bluntness of the question, but she replied evenly, "None of those. But I'm sure you're not really interested in my private life, Mr. Riddell."

He sat forward and looked at her intently. "Oh, but perhaps I am. Perhaps I'm very interested. Tell me about your private life, Miss Holly Weston, tell me all about it. I want to hear every detail—who was your first lover; how many men you've been to bed with; who cured you of being a romantic. Come, tell me all about yourself," he commanded with a definitely nasty edge to his voice.

Holly frowned, not pretending that she hadn't understood where he was heading. "I haven't asked you any questions about your personal life, Mr. Riddell."

"No, but that's why you came here, isn't it? To

probe and pry into my past, to hold an autopsy on my marriages, find out about my business interests. And most of all, of course, to find out why I shut myself away on this island. That's the truth now, isn't it?" he demanded forcefully, his fist hitting the table.

For a long moment Holly looked back at him without speaking, then she said slowly, "That was the story I came to Greece to get, yes. But only if you had chosen to give it to me of your own free will. Since it turns out that it wasn't you who had agreed to an interview, then I have no right to ask you any questions, and I won't do so."

He stared at her for long seconds, complete surprise on his face. "A reporter with moral scruples— I don't believe it!"

"I work for a very reputable journal, Mr. Riddell, not one of the sensationalist newspapers. We would have checked every fact that I'd been given before we published the story." She smiled thinly. "Somehow I doubt if either my paper or you would have been very pleased if we'd had banner headlines branding you as a deformed idiot."

A look of horror came over his face. "Good God, no!"

"Although," Holly added thoughtfully, "it would have forced you to repudiate it. You'd have had to come out into the open then."

"So I would. Perhaps we've both had a lucky escape." He looked at her keenly. "So you're really not going to ask me any questions?"

She shook her head, smiling, but adding provocatively, "Not unless you want to tell me, of course.

But, you know, you're going to have to tell your story sometime. Those men could easily have duped a reporter who hadn't done his homework thoroughly. And—I don't know how much you keep in touch with gossip columns and the like—but there have been a great many rumors going around about you lately: that you're a drug addict, recovering from a nervous breakdown, that you're imp—'' She stopped herself hurriedly and tried to cover the hesitation by adding quickly, "Some even say that you've died and that a consortium is running your business. Which could be very bad for your stockmarket shareholdings if it gained any ground.''

Felix Riddell shrugged dismissivley. "Those kinds of rumors have been circulating almost since the day I moved here. I'll know how to deal with them if they start to get out of proportion." His eyes fixed on her steadily. "But there was one rumor that you changed your mind about telling me; what was it?"

To her annoyance Holly found herself starting to blush. "Oh, it was nothing, really."

"Then tell me," he commanded in a tone that brooked no denial.

"Well—" she looked down at the table, tracing along the edge of it with her finger "—well, they, er, they did sort of mention that you might be impotent."

She had expected him to be angry but to her surprise he laughed heartily. Leaning forward, he reached out to cover her hand with his. His eyebrows rose and there was a look in his eyes that Holly couldn't fail to understand. "I can assure you

Take these 4 best-selling Harlequin romance stories FREE

exciting details inside

that that's one rumor that is definitely untrue. In fact, I'll be pleased to prove it to you personally if you'll give me the chance?"

Before Holly could even begin to form an answer they were interrupted by the sound of footsteps and Felix Riddell turned around, a frown on his face, but his hand still holding hers. There were three men crossing the patio toward them—two of them were holding guns that were steadily trained on the third man, who was obviously their prisoner. Holly took one look at the third man and froze into a stunned silence.

Felix Riddell demanded angrily, "Who the hell is this? How did he get here?"

One of the men with the guns answered tersely, "He sailed his boat into the bay. We warned him off but he kept right on coming, even though we fired at him. He says he's come for the girl," he added, nodding toward Holly.

"But I see that I needn't have worried," Nick spoke for the first time, his tone heavy with sarcasm as he looked pointedly at their joined hands.

Holly hastily drew hers away and put it under the table.

Riddell looked from Nick's face to hers. He stood up. "Do you know him?" he asked her.

Nodding reluctantly, she replied, "Yes, he's the Englishman I told you about."

"Ah, yes." He addressed the two men. "It's all right, you can go. But later I will want an explanation from you two on how he managed to land here." This was said with a frown that bode them no good, and the men's shoulders sagged as they left. Turning back to Nick he said, "So you thought she needed rescuing, did you?" He moved around to stand in front of Nick, drawing himself up to his full height. Both of them were tall men and well built, but the years of dissipation had begun to show on Riddell, in the slight thickening of his waistline and the lines around his eyes, whereas Nick had still the suppleness and vigor of youth. An instantaneous antagonism seemed to have sprung up between the two, and it seemed to Holly that they faced each other like boxers squaring away for a fight, or a king stag preparing to defend his ground and his harem of does from a challenging newcomer.

Sarcastically Riddell added, "And so you decided to do your Sir Galahad act to impress the lady." He glanced at Holly, asking, "Are you impressed?"

Nick, too, turned to look at her, and Holly found that she couldn't have answered for the life of her.

His lips twisting into a cynical smile, Nick said, "It seems that I wasted my time. The lady only needs saving from herself."

"So why don't you take yourself and your boat back where you came from," Riddell said harshly. "I'll bring Miss Weston back when she's ready to go. And in future when you're warned off, stay off."

Nick put his hands in the pockets of his jeans and leaned nonchalantly against the table. "Either she comes with me or we both stay."

Riddell's brows drew into an angry frown. "Do you want me to have you thrown out?"

His voice silky but holding a definite challenge,

Nick said, "Go ahead and send for your henchmen and let them try—if you can't do it yourself, that is."

Projecting herself into the sudden tension, Holly said hastily, "I'm quite ready to go now. I'm sorry that I intruded on you, Mr. Riddell, but thank you for lending me the clothes. I'll send them back to you just as soon as I get to Kinos."

He drew his eyes away from Nick's to look at her. "Keep them," he said briefly. Then he said persuasively, "There's no need for you to go yet, Holly. I told you I'd put a motor boat at your disposal. Why don't you stay and have lunch with me? Maybe we can talk some more about why you came here."

Holly looked at him quickly, hopefully, wondering if he was considering letting her do an interview after all.

Seeing the gleam of interest in her gray eyes, Felix smiled down at her, the lazily seductive smile that had won his countless conquests in the past. "Why don't you tell our well-meaning but extremely interfering friend here to take off?"

Before she could answer, Nick stepped forward and put a hand on her shoulder in the age-old possessive gesture of a male for his mate. "Perhaps the situation hasn't been made quite clear to you," he said, addressing the older man and looking him straight in the eyes. "The lady happens to be my wife."

There was a short, rather shattering silence, and then Riddell looked at her and said coldly, "Is this true? Are you married to him?"

Her face pale except for two bright spots of color

high on her cheekbones, Holly answered steadily, "In theory."

Felix Riddell's eyes sharpened. "But not in practice?"

Even with Nick's fingers biting deeply into her shoulder, she replied with a firm, "No."

CHAPTER FIVE

HOLLY CAREFULLY REFRAINED from saying a word until she and Nick had been escorted down to the small harbor by the two guards and had boarded his boat and were sailing back toward Kinos, but all the time her anger and resentment at his high-handed action was steadily growing. Nick, too, had kept a tight-lipped silence as he went about the business of raising the sails and steering them away from Fallipos. He had removed his hand from her shoulder the moment she had denied him, but he had still refused to go without her, so there had been nothing for her to do but to leave at once. There was no way the two men could have spent any more time together without there being a nasty confrontation of some sort or another.

The wind filled the dull red of the sails as they passed out of the protecting arms of the harbor bay, setting the rigging creaking and the waves lapping merrily against the sleek hull, but Holly was oblivious to the music of the sea and the wind. She was entirely caught up in her own emotions and turned on Nick furiously.

"How *dare* you come for me? Just what right do you think you have after all these years to just walk in and start interfering in my life? I could have *killed* you!"

Nick laughed unpleasantly. "Spoiled your pitch, did I, Holly? And just as you were getting really friendly with the great man, too. From the look of it he was just on the point of propositioning you when I turned up."

This was so near the truth, even though she was sure that Felix Riddell had only been funning, that Holly felt herself start to color guiltily. Which, of course, only served to make her angrier than ever. "Whether he was or not is none of your damned business. How I lead my life is my own affair. You gave up any right you might have had to question it the day you walked out on me."

Nick's dark brows drew into a frown. "You're quite right—what you do doesn't concern me. I came to find you only because your paper has been calling you since dawn this morning. The hotel keeper had seen us together and when he found that you hadn't slept in your room last night, he came over to my boat to see if you were with me." He smiled thinly. "After I explained that I was the last person you would have spent the night with, he told me that your paper wanted to get in touch with you urgently, and he asked me to take the call because his English isn't that fluent. It seems they were afraid you might have been duped by the person you were supposed to meet. Your editor had found out that a trick had been tried before or something, and he wanted to catch you before you fell for it." His eyes ran over her, noting that her clothes were different from the ones she'd worn the day before. "I take it that your being out all night means that you did fall for it?"

Holly glared at him. "Well, that's just where you're wrong. They were very clever, but I saw through them."

"So how come you end up by being with Felix Riddell?"

For a moment she opened her mouth to tell him the whole story, but then hesitated; even though she'd seen through the imposture, she had a pretty good idea that Nick would still condemn her as a fool for putting herself in such a dangerous position, especially when he heard that she'd fallen overboard and had to swim for it. No, somehow the less he or anyone else knew about it, the better. So she merely replied shortly, "I've already told you that it's none of your business," and turned to see how far they were from Kinos.

But the mocking tone in which he said, "Afraid to tell me?" brought her sharply around to face him again.

"No, I'm *not* afraid to tell you. I just don't choose to, that's all," she snapped, furious again. "If you hadn't barged in when you did I might even have persuaded Felix Riddell to give me his story."

"Yes, I noticed how persuasive you were being," Nick agreed dryly. "Who was doing the propositioning, him or you?" His tone grew insulting. "Or was he just thanking you for spending last night with him?"

"Why you...." Overcome with rage, Holly

sprang to her feet, took two furious steps across the deck, and before Nick could stop her, hit him hard across the face! Her anger at the present situation had triggered it off, but behind the slap was the pent-up hurt and resentment of the last seven years. Bitterness welled up like a flood and once started she couldn't stop. "You louse! You swine!" With every epithet she hit out at him blindly, wanting to hurt, to give as much pain as she had suffered.

Her first blow had taken him by surprise, but then Nick raised his right arm to defend himself, his left hand still holding the wheel as he tried to steer the boat and capture her flailing hands. Then he gave a curse and let go of the wheel completely so that the boat yawed and came around, the sail flapping emptily against the mast.

"You little spitfire!"

He reached out to grab her, but she was in such a blind fury, beating against his chest with her fists, trying to claw at his face, that it took a few minutes for him to catch her wrists and twist them behind her back. Even then Holly still struggled and fought; twisting in his arms and arching her body as she sought vainly to get free. She began to butt him in the face, and Nick swore savagely and wound a hand in her hair, jerking her head away so sharply that she winced with sudden pain.

"Damn you, you little wildcat! Stop it!" He shook her then, roughly, his voice as angry as her own. And when he let her go she stood before him, no longer fighting but trembling with spent rage and emotion, tears running unhindered down her cheeks. As Nick looked at her he gave a strange, strangled sort of groan. "Oh, God, Holly!" And then he pulled her roughly, almost violently to him and kissed her devouringly, his fingers digging into her arms, his lips bruising hers as he took her mouth with a savage intensity, not caring whether he hurt her or not.

"No!" She tried to pull away, horrified at what was happening, but he dragged her back hard against him and put his arm down to hold her body close, while he put the other hand at the back of her neck so that she couldn't turn her head away from the cruel ravishment of his mouth. It was impossible to break free, so Holly tried to hold herself rigid, to disassociate herself from his embrace, but then the harder fight began as memories started to flood back; the strong hardness of his lips that had caressed her body so many times, the sharp tang of the after-shave he had always worn, the sheer animal masculinity of him; all the evocative sensations that had lain dormant in her subconscious, deliberately pushed out of mind for so long, came back now to fill her with all the sensual desire that his kisses had always aroused in her. It had always been like this. Right from the very first she had never been able to resist him when he set out to arouse her, soon capitulating and moaning with desire as his hands and lips explored her, caressed her.

With a choking cry, Holly tore herself from Nick's arms, her hands going up across her chest as if to protect herself from him. "You rotten swine. Take your filthy hands off me!"

Nick gazed at her, his breath ragged and uneven, his face for a moment naked and vulnerable, then he seemed to make a conscious effort to pull himself together. "You had that coming," he said harshly. "You've been asking for it since the moment we met."

"That's where you're wrong," Holly reneged. "It's the last thing I want from you."

Nick's jaw tightened. "You wanted it once. You used to almost beg me to make love to you." His voice became grim. "But then that was all I could give you, wasn't it? Your parents made sure of that."

Unevenly Holly said, "Leave my parents out of this. What they did—" she shrugged tiredly "—is over and best forgotten."

Nick looked at her sharply. "You know, then, that it was their interference that split us up?"

She nodded. "Yes, I realized soon after you'd gone."

"We might never have parted if it hadn't been for them."

Holly smiled bitterly. "Oh, I'm quite sure we would. If you cared for me so little that you could just walk away and never even try to write or contact me in any way, then I'm quite sure that our marriage wouldn't have lasted much longer than it did, in any circumstances."

While she spoke Nick had been looking at her searchingly, but now he took a hasty step toward her. "Holly, I . . . ."

But she moved away and said quickly, "Nick, let's leave it, *please*. It all happened so long ago. It's over and done with now. What's the use of tearing each other apart, raking it all up again?"

He stared down at her for a long moment, then said slowly, "Does it ... tear you apart?"

Holly tried to turn her head away from his searching gaze, not answering, but he put his hand up to her chin and forced her to face him. "Does it, Holly?" he asked again, a note almost of urgency in his voice.

She tried to read his face, to find out what he wanted her to say. Did he want her to say yes because it would give him sadistic delight to know that he still had the power to rouse her emotions, or did he genuinely want to know? Holly found that she wasn't prepared to give so much of herself away, and countered with, "Does it you?"

The urgent light died out of his eyes and he let her go and stepped back. He smiled without humor. "As I said, women are always afraid to answer a direct question." Then he turned abruptly away and went back to the wheel of the boat, ignoring her.

Holly turned with a sigh of relief to lean over the rail and watch the outline of Kinos gradually come nearer. It was true that she had realized that her parents had been responsible for the breakup of their marriage soon after Nick had left, but that hadn't been the direct reason. At first, in the first week or so after Nick had gone, she had been positive that he would either come back, or else that he would have found them somewhere else to live and insist that she join him, but as the days had gone by and there had been no word from him, her parents had started to talk of divorce, taking it for granted that she would agree. The bitter realization that he had indeed left her stunned her so much that Holly hardly realized what they were saying. It was only when they went over her head and made her an appointment with the family lawyer, that Holly came to her senses. By then she knew that she was pregnant and told them, expecting them to drop all talk of a divorce and do their best to help her find Nick so that they could try to patch things up. But to her horror, her parents' reaction was that it made no difference—she must go ahead with the divorce and have an abortion. As her mother said, "You surely don't want that ungrateful upstart's child? Not after what he's done to you ... and to us?"

Bitter scenes had followed then, with her parents trying to persuade, and when that didn't work, to bully her into having an abortion. But Holly had been adamant in her stand, hoping, but with ever increasing despair, that Nick would contact her. After several weeks, when hope had at last died and her parents' continual nagging became intolerable, she had packed her clothes, drawn what little money she had out of the bank, and grimly left their house to live in a tatty, one-roomed bed-sitter in London. At first it hadn't been too bad—she had found a job as a waitress in a hamburger bar quite easily, but as her pregnancy progressed and became obvious, her movements slower, she had been dismissed and had to rely on unemployment insurance to live. She had let her father know her address, as much in the forlorn hope that Nick would get in touch with her, as anything, but they had made no attempt to contact her or come to see her, and when she wrote again to let them know that they had become grandparents, the letter was returned marked No Longer at This Address. There had been times then, when she was cold and hungry, afraid to let the baby cry in case she got thrown out by her landlady, that she had hated her parents for not standing by her, but with the new maturity thrust upon her she had come to realize that it was her own stubbornness that had brought her down. If she wanted to keep her baby, then she would have to rely on her own resources.

Of Nick she tried not to think at all. Knowing now of her parents' deliberate campaign against him, she could understand why he had left and forgive him for it, but nothing could make her forgive him for not caring what happened to her after he had gone, for not trying to make a go of their marriage outside her parents' home.

She turned now to look at him, standing tall at the wheel, his hair ruffled by the breeze. It had been a hard and bitter struggle to keep and rear his child. She wondered suddenly what he would say, what he would do if he knew, if she came right out now and told him. Holly smiled grimly to herself; he would probably take her back to Kinos as fast as he could and then turn around and get the hell back to Australia or wherever he was going without a moment's pause, rather than have even the possibility of being saddled with a wife and child he didn't want. The smile became even more bitter. Maybe he might even ask the classic question, "Who's the lucky father?" But as she watched him he lifted his head to look up at the pennant flying at the top of the mast and her heart gave a dizzying lurch; there was no need to ask who Jamie's father was. He tilted his head in exactly the same way as Nick when he looked up at her, with the same long-lashed blue eyes and the firm, determined chin. No one, seeing them together, would ever question his parentage.

Nick turned his head and caught her watching him. His eyes met hers and held them steadily until the memory of that bruising kiss came vividly back and Holly dropped hers, a slight flush of color in her cheeks. He said, "Will you be going back to England now that your assignment is over?"

"Yes, there's nothing here to stay for now," she agreed stiltedly. "I'll leave tomorrow morning."

He shook his head. "There isn't another ferry until Wednesday. You'll have a couple of days to wait." He hesitated, then said, "I was thinking of making a trip sometime to Samos, an island about half a day's sailing from here. Pythagoras, the mathematician, was born there, and you can see the remains of the temple of Hera, one of the seven wonders of the ancient world. If you like we could go tomorrow, spend the night there, and sail back the day after so that you can catch the ferry on Wednesday."

Thrown by his sudden invitation, Holly said bluntly, "Why on earth do you want to take me?"

Nick shrugged. "You're at a loose end and I thought it might amuse you."

Holly sniffed disparagingly. "I would hardly think it would be amusing to spend so much time in each other's close company when we can't even exchange two sentences without ripping into one another."

Keeping his voice level, Nick said, "Maybe we ought to give it a try for that very reason. To see why we have this effect on each other."

"But that's obvious," Holly returned with a frown. "It's because of what happened between us in the past, of course."

"Is it! Seven years is a hell of a long time, Holly. I was just a student then, and you little more than a schoolgirl. We've both changed, become adults. The bad times we went through then shouldn't have lasted to color our emotions now. Not," he added slowly, "unless they went very deep. And if they did that, then they must have mattered a lot— to both of us."

He had been looking at her steadily as he spoke and it was this, as much as his words, that silenced the harsh retort Holly had been planning to make. Instead she turned away and looked blindly out to sea. "I . . . I don't know," she stammered.

"Think about it. Maybe if we talked the thing through . . . ."

But Holly broke in sharply. "No! What's the point in holding an inquest now? The corpse is already rotten in its grave!"

Nick was silent for a moment. Then he said rather flatly, "All right. If that's the way you want it. So just come along for the ride."

"I don't know," she said again. "I'll have to think about it."

They were silent then until they sailed into Melmia harbor and Nick had moored the boat. He vaulted lightly over the rail onto the wall and then reached down to give her a hand, but she stumbled as the boat moved under her and he had to catch hold of her to prevent her falling, lifting her bodily onto the quay.

"Oh," She gave a gasp as she found herself held close against him, his arm firmly around her waist.

For a moment he continued to hold her, his eyes on her face so close to his own. Holly thought for a few crazy seconds that he was going to kiss her again and stiffened, but he merely said brusquely, "I'll be at the *taverna* at eight tonight. You can tell me then whether or not you want to go to Samos tomorrow."

He released her then, so suddenly that she was taken by surprise. Giving her a curt nod of farewell, Nick jumped back on board and began to busy himself in folding the sails.

Holly began to walk slowly back to the *taverna*, her heart still racing in her chest. Her thoughts went back to the fight on the boat. Nick had said then that she had asked for it, inferring that she'd deliberately started the fight to provoke him into finishing it the way he had. But that wasn't true at all, at least not consciously; all she had wanted then was to hurt him. And when he had started to kiss her she had resisted by every means in her power. It was only as it went on that it had evoked memories of the good times, the wonderful, halcyon times when he had made such ardent love to her. Then, too, he had been uncontrolled, his desire for her overriding everything else as he had taken her in a frenzy of wild passion that had raised them both to the heights of physical ecstasy. Even now, just thinking about it still had the power to make her skin prickle with heat, to send waves of sensuality and longing coursing through her body.

Holly came to a sudden stop, cursing herself for a fool. She was behaving like a bitter, frustrated spinster, relying on fantasies for her kicks. And that's all it was, really, a fantasy—something that happened so long ago and for such a short time that it had taken on a dreamlike quality. Or had, until Nick had brought it all so rudely back to reality, to the present instead of the dim and distant past. Brought it back so vividly that when he had helped her off the boat and held her in his arms she had wanted him to kiss her, wanted urgently to feel his mouth on hers, to have his hands touch her until he had roused her to the peak of desire, to.... Holly shuddered, forcing her mind away. Such thoughts were the height of madness. This was the man who had walked out on her and that was all that mattered. That fact, and only that, was what she must remember, hold in her mind. Everything else must be firmly shut out. Both for her own sake and that of her little son, she must not let ancient memories of shared joy intrude into her life now. The path she had chosen was a lone one and didn't include any permanent male companion ... and not for a moment would it include Nick Falconer! She had given herself to him in love and trust once, but she would never do so again.

But there was still the problem of the expedition to Samos to be worked out. Had his motives been purely altruistic? Somehow Holly couldn't see it, any more than she could understand why Nick sought her out or had come after her to Felix Riddell's island. It couldn't be possessiveness or jealousy; if he'd felt those emotions he would never have left her in the first place. Although the way he had squared up to the millionaire had definitely had a "hands off, this is mine" belligerence about it. Holly sighed. Drat Nick Falconer. Why did he have to come back into her life, she thought grimly. In fact, why had he ever come into it at all? But that thought brought her up short; if there had been no Nick, there would be no Jamie. But apart from that.... Holly paused outside the *taverna* and turned to look back at the boat where Nick was reefing the last sail. No, she knew now, in a sudden blinding revelation, that despite all the grief and pain that had come after, not for anything would she have missed those few ecstatic months when they had been lovers.

Going into the *taverna*, Holly told the relieved Alexis Lambis that she was quite safe and then went up to her room to change out of the clothes Felix Riddell had loaned her. He'd said she could keep them, of course, but she was determined to return them. Even if he only had the things thrown in the garbage, at least her conscience would be clear. Her mouth puckered into a *moue* of chagrin at the failure of her assignment. And worse than that, she had lost all her precious camera equipment. She could just imagine the editor's face when she told him, and her spirits sank dejectedly. The paper would provide her with new equipment, of course, but the editor wouldn't be pleased, especially as she didn't even have a story to justify the loss. And when he heard that she had actually met Riddell and not got an interview out of him, he'd probably hit the roof!

She slept through most of the afternoon, then went down to the beach to swim and sunbathe for an hour or so before getting changed for dinner. During that time she had thought of little else but Nick's invitation, but even when she went down at eight to meet him, she still hadn't made up her mind. One minute she thought that she would accept, to prove to herself that she was immune to him as much as anything, the next she decided that she couldn't, that she was still far too vulnerable to him and being alone with him for two days would be bound to lead to disaster one way or another. Quite which way her mind shrank from pursuing. If he hadn't kissed her on the boat everything would have been clear cut; she definitely wouldn't have gone with him because they argued all the time, but now...now there was a fatal fascination about the idea. Holly knew there ought not to be, knew that the only sane thing to do was to stop short right now and have nothing more to do with Nick, to just keep out of his way until she could leave the island. But that kiss had left her weak and confused, incapable of making a decision, her body filled with a yearning that she thought had died long ago.

Nick was waiting for her at one of the tables on the terrace, wearing a lightweight tan safari suit this time. He stood up as she walked toward him, looking at her appraisingly. Holly found that she couldn't meet his eyes and sat down hurriedly, making a business of arranging the stole she'd brought with her around her shoulders until she'd had time to collect herself a little and could face him with a degree of composure.

Holly was afraid that he would come straight out and ask her for her decision, but thankfully he just asked her what she wanted to eat and then told her something of his job, explaining what he did and where it had taken him during the last seven years. Then it was her turn to talk about her work, her face becoming animated as she did so, her hands expressively emphasizing her point.

They continued to talk on safe, uncontroversial subjects while they ate, but afterward Nick subtly brought it back to a more personal level.

"You've obviously been quite a success in your career. What made you take it up in the first place? I don't remember you ever wanting to when we were together."

"No." Holly picked up her glass of wine and ran her finger idly around the edge. "I decided to take it up soon after . . . you went away."

They were both silent for a moment until Nick said, "But why photojournalism?"

"It was just journalism at first—the photography came later when I had more time." She hesitated, then said, "I needed something that I could do mostly at home, that gave me some free time to attend to . . . other things."

"Like the full social life you've always been used to," Nick interrupted sardonically. "All the cocktail parties, dances and coffee mornings you couldn't live without."

Holly's chin came up. "Of course. What else?" she retorted in cold sarcasm.

A puzzled look came into his blue eyes. "What did your parents think of your work? It wasn't exactly what they had in mind for you, was it? They approved wholeheartedly of the social-butterfly existence you were living."

Holly became interested in her glass again. "They had nothing to do with it. In fact, they knew nothing about it." She shrugged. "They probably still don't. You see I ... I left home shortly after you did. I haven't seen my parents since."

Nick stared at her incredulously. "You left home? But didn't they try to stop you? You were only seventeen, still under-age, surely they—"

"You forget," Holly interrupted tightly, "they were no longer my legal guardians—you were. And as you weren't around to express your wishes on the subject ..." She let the sentence tail off, the words she hadn't said as expressive as those she had.

Nick was still staring at her, his mouth drawn into a thin line. Heavily he said, "Why, Holly? Why did you leave home? Was it because of what had happened to us, because you realized that it was your parents who had—" he paused "—who had come between us?"

"Who had made life intolerable for you, you mean, don't you?" She sat back in her chair and looked out to sea, at the water lapping gently on the shore, curling in soft waves of phosphorescence in the moonlight, as she wondered how much to tell him. Slowly she answered, "It was partly that, but there were ... other things."

"What other things, Holly?" he said insistently when she didn't go on.

Speaking with difficulty, she replied, "They...
they wanted me to get a divorce straightaway—but I
refused. There were rows, so I left."

Nick tensed and sat forward, his eyes on her face
intently. "Why didn't you want a divorce?"

"Because I...." Her hand began to shake and
Holly hastily set down the glass. She would have
put her hand in her lap, under the table out of sight,
but before she could do so, Nick reached quickly
out and covered it with his, holding it firmly so that
she couldn't escape. She raised eyes that were suddenly afraid. "Please, Nick. I don't want to talk
about it anymore." She tried to pull her hand away,
but he wouldn't let go.

"No, Holly, you can't stop now. *You have to go
on*. Why didn't you want a divorce?"

Holly stared at him, unable to hide her vulnera-
bility. "Because I.... At first, you see I...I thought
you would come back." His hand tightened on
hers, tightened until it hurt. Biting her lip, she
looked away and was silent for a long moment.
Then, her voice changing completely, becoming
harsh and bitter, she went on, "And then, when I
was sure that you weren't, that you had gone for
good, there was no point in getting a divorce."
Adding venomously, "What would be the use of
being free when I had no intention of ever marry-
ing again? I may have been fool enough to marry
you, but not such a fool that I didn't learn by my
mistake. If nothing else those few months with you
taught me never to put my trust in a man again!"

Shaking with emotion, she glared across at Nick,
but he was staring at her with a strange, almost be-

mused expression in his eyes. Leaning forward across the table, he said urgently, "Holly, *you* never got a divorce; has it ever occurred to you to wonder why *I* didn't?"

She smiled crookedly. "Only once. And when I realized what the answer must be I certainly didn't want to think about it anymore."

His eyebrows rose. "Just what answer did you come up with?"

"The right one. That it was convenient for you to remain married because it was a way out of any entanglements with women who wanted to tie you down, who weren't satisfied with just an affair and wanted to make it permanent," she answered curtly.

An angry glint came into his eyes for a moment, and she felt his fingers tighten on her hand again, but then he relaxed and said, "And did it never occur to you that you might be wrong? That my reasons for not getting a divorce could be identical to your own?" He hesitated, then said slowly, "That they might even go further than that?"

Holly stared at him, her throat feeling suddenly tight. "What...what do you mean?" she stammered.

Earnestly he said, "Holly, I didn't just walk out on you. I did ...."

"Excuse me, Miss Weston?"

Holly looked up rather dazedly to see a man in a dark, naval-looking uniform standing by the table. Vaguely she was aware of Nick's furious "Hell and damnation!" as he let go of her hand.

"Y-yes, I'm Holly Weston."

The man gave a courteous little bow. "I am in

the employ of Mr. Riddell, madame. He asked me to bring this to you." He held out her bag of photographic gear and her cassette recorder, thankfully still intact.

"Oh, you found it! Oh, how wonderful." Holly's face lighted with pleasure and relief. Without thinking she added, "I was sure those men would have thrown it overboard after me."

"No, madame, it was found safely aboard the yacht." He took a white envelope from his pocket and held it out to her. "Mr. Riddell also asked me to give you this letter and to wait for your answer."

Holly took it from him and slid open the envelope, aware, without actually looking directly at him, that Nick was frowning in disapproval. The letter was brief and to the point.

"You may well be right about me having to come clean with my story. Why not come over to Fallipos tomorrow so that we can discuss it further. Yours, Felix Riddell."

Hardly able to believe her good fortune, Holly didn't hesitate before turning to the messenger. "Please tell Mr. Riddell that the answer is yes, I'd be pleased to visit him tomorrow."

"Very well, madame. The yacht will call for you at ten tomorrow morning, if that is convenient for you?"

"That will be fine. Thank you."

The man gave another small bow and left them alone again.

His voice tight, Nick said, "I take it that means you won't be coming with me to Samos tomorrow after all?"

"No. I'm sorry, Nick, but as you've probably guessed there's a possibility that Felix Riddell may give me an interview ... and I can't afford to pass up a chance like that."

"Not even for a prior engagement?"

She looked at him steadily. "I hadn't said that I'd definitely go with you, Nick."

"No more you had." He sat back, anger in his eyes, his tone heavy with contempt. "So instead you're going over to Fallipos. Running to do Felix Riddell's bidding when he crooks his little finger at you. And will you be just as willing to meet his terms for an interview?"

Holly's face paled. "And just exactly what do you mean by that?"

"You know darn well what I mean! Just what lengths are you willing to go to to get this story?"

Angrily Holly got to her feet, but Nick reached out and caught her arm. "Oh, no, you're not running away from this one." Exerting his strength he forced her down into her chair again. Holly glared at him in impotent fury, angry as much with her own weakness as with him. "Let go of me, you swine!"

Nick grinned maliciously. "Not until I'm good and ready. I'm beginning to realize just how much you've changed. Tell me, where did they teach you to prostitute yourself for a story—at the School of Journalism?"

"How *dare* you!" Holly's eyes blazed. "For your information, I've never, *never* had to use sex to get a story ... and I don't intend to start now!"

"No?" he asked jeeringly. "When I found you with Felix Riddell you were holding hands and definitely *not* behaving like strangers who had just met."

Shrugging rather helplessly, Holly said, "That was just . . . just a joke. A reaction to something I'd asked him." Nick's eyebrows rose in disbelief, and she added fiercely, "Believe it or not. I couldn't care less. I don't have to defend myself to you. And just because we happened to live under the same roof for a few months certainly doesn't give you the right to question me now."

"And shared the same bed. Don't forget that!" Nick interrupted grimly.

That silenced Holly as nothing else would have done. She stared at him for a long moment, her eyes large in her pale face, then she blinked and looked down, putting up her free hand to lean her head on it.

He released the grip on her arm, moving his hand down to cover hers as he said urgently, "Holly, please don't go to see Felix Riddell tomorrow. Come with me to Samos instead."

She started to shake her head. "There wouldn't be any point. We have nothing to say to each other and—"

But he broke in quickly. "Yes, there is, Holly. I've a great deal to tell you that you don't know. Things that could make all the difference to us."

"No," she answered firmly. "I came here to do a job and that must come first. I'm not here on holiday like you. I have responsibilities even if you haven't."

His eyebrows rose in surprise. "What responsibilities?"

Biting her lip, Holly hastily covered her slip by saying, "To my paper, of course. They pay me to go after stories, not to pass them up because I've received an invitation to go sailing. And if they heard that I'd let slip an opportunity like this, they'd probably fire me."

Nick took his hand from hers and sat back in his chair. "Would you like another drink?"

"No. No, thanks." Holly shook her head, glad that he seemed to have taken no for an answer at last. For a few minutes they sat in a rather strained silence, Nick looking broodingly out to sea while Holly wondered just what it was that he had wanted to tell her, things he'd said she hadn't known, that could make all the difference to them. Briefly she wondered if he had just made it up as a lure to persuade her to go with him, but then she dismissed the idea from her mind; whatever else he had been, Nick had never been devious. Always in the past he had been completely open and aboveboard, had never tried to deceive her in any way. So if he said he had something to tell her.... She opened her mouth to ask him what it was but he forestalled her.

"What did you mean when that man of Riddell's gave you your gear back and you said you were afraid it had followed you overboard?"

Holly looked discomfitted. "Oh, that. It was nothing." She glanced at his watch and gave a pretended gasp of surprise. "Good heavens. Eleventhirty already." Standing up, she picked up her case and nodded to him. "Thanks for the meal, Nick. Sorry I can't make it tomorrow. I expect you'll be moving on soon, so I'll say goodbye as well as good night in case I don't see you again." Then she gave him a bright, false smile before walking quickly away.

He hadn't said anything, just watched her go, although Holly half expected him to try and stop her. He merely sat there silently drawing on his cigarette, his expression completely unreadable.

It was almost with a sense of release that Holly shut the door of her room and dropped her case on the table. She supposed that she ought to check its contents, but it would have to wait until the morning; right now she was too tired to bother, her complete lack of sleep the previous night hitting her now. And the last few hours with Nick hadn't helped; she had been as tense as a coiled spring, unable to relax, her emotions like trip wires ready to be set off by the slightest jar. Only now that she was away from his menacing presence could she start to unwind, to sit on her bed and lean back against the wall, eyes closed, hands shaking a little from the release of tension.

The rap on her door broke sharply into her almost trancelike state. More asleep than awake, Holly automatically got up to answer it, only briefly wondering who it could be. But when she opened the door and saw Nick leaning his long length against the door jamb, she came fully awake in an instant. Immediately she moved to slam the door in his face, but he put his foot out to stop her and then calmly pushed his way in and closed the door behind him.

Eyes blazing, she said furiously, "If you don't get out of here this minute I'll start screaming for help!"

Nick's left eyebrow rose sardonically. "Go ahead—but don't forget that we're in a still rather primitive area of Greece. The people here have very basic ideas about what rights a man has over his wife ... and one of them is definitely visiting her bedroom whenever he feels like it."

"They don't know I'm your wife. I don't use your name anymore," Holly broke in heatedly.

"But they will when I show them the photograph I have in my wallet; you in your virginal white and me in the morning suit your parents insisted on," he explained tauntingly.

Holly's face paled. "You ... you still carry that around with you?"

"You never know when it might come in handy."

"I can imagine!" she retorted sarcastically, but then looked away, feeling totally confused. Haltingly, she said, "Why have you come here, Nick?"

He didn't answer immediately, but waited for her to look at him again, to see the lazy, mocking smile on his lips before he lifted his arm from where it had been partly hidden at his side and held her stole out to her. "You left this behind. It fell off the back of your chair."

"Oh! I ... I see." She moved forward slowly and reached out to take it from him, then stopped suddenly.

Nick's eyes gazed down into hers, the mockery gone from them now and in its place an entirely different light. Softly he said, "Come here."

Holly began to tremble and she said in a stammering entreaty, "No, Nick. Please, no."

But he let the stole fall to the floor and put his hands on her shoulders to gently draw her toward him. He kissed her slowly, deliberately, exploring her mouth with his lips in tiny little kisses that made her insides seem to take fire. She gave a little moan under her breath and stirred sensuously, moving closer to him, but he held her off, not letting her get too near. Then his right hand left her shoulder and began to move downward, caressing her neck, her breast and on down to her hips. Desire grew, filling her body with intense yearning, and she began to writhe under his hand. His kiss became more passionate then, his tongue touching her lips as she opened her mouth under his. Suddenly he put both his hands low on her hips and pulled her hard against him, letting her know how much he wanted her. Holly gasped as she felt his hard body against hers, heard him groan deep in his throat as she put her arms around his neck and pressed herself against him, returning his kisses with a fierce hunger.

His hand moved up to twine itself in her hair, his lips bruising, but then he pulled her head away so that he could see her face.

His voice thick and unsteady, he said softly, "It was always good between us, Holly. Whatever else was wrong, this was always perfect. Even the very first time, when you were still a virgin; it was one of the most wonderful experiences of my life. And it was for you, too, wasn't it? Wasn't it?" he repeated, his head coming down to kiss her neck, her throat, his breath burning her skin.

"Yes," she moaned softly. "You know it was."

He sought her lips again, compulsively, his dominant sexuality demanding submission. "I want to make love to you, my darling one," he murmured against her mouth. "Just the way it used to be."

It may have been that last phrase, or perhaps the endearment, one that he had never used when they were together, that brought Holly back to reality, that made her suddenly shiver as if she was very cold and deliberately move out of his arms. He looked down at her in surprise, his eyes dark with desire, his pulse unsteady.

Tightly she said, "I think you got it wrong, didn't you? You don't mean make love at all; you mean that you just want to have sex with me. Because that's all it would be."

"No, Holly, that isn't so." Nick took a hasty step toward her, his hands reaching out for her, but she backed away.

"No?" Her voice became jeering, bitter. "What are you trying to tell me, then? That you never stopped loving me, or that now you've seen me you've fallen in love with me all over again?"

Nick's hands dropped to his sides. Slowly he said, "Something like that, yes."

Holly laughed jarringly. "You must be crazy if you expect me to believe that. The way I read it, if you'd loved me you'd never have left me. People don't just walk out on those they love—not if they really care about them. But perhaps you didn't know that. Perhaps you thought I'd just fall into your arms the way I did before. Well, all right, I admit that you can still turn me on. And that's all you want really, isn't it?" Her voice unsteady, she faced up to him. "For some crazy reason you just want to prove to yourself that you can still make me. That after all these years you still have the power to dominate me sexually." She looked up into his eyes, glacier cold now, and shivered convulsively again. "Okay, so I admit it," she repeated, her voice rising. "So why don't you ...."

But Nick stepped forward and caught her by the elbows jerking her toward him. "But I haven't, have I? Not yet."

She stared up at him, suddenly frightened. "What ... what do you mean?"

"You know exactly what I mean. Even though I excite you, you're letting your head rule you so that you back off at the last minute. You're a coward, Holly. You're willing to make verbal submission in the hope that I'll be satisfied and leave you alone, but you're afraid to give yourself to me in case you find out that what you feel for me is more than just physical need."

"That's all it could possibly be," Holly broke in defiantly. "That's all it ever was!"

"Was it?" Nick's brows rose as he let her go. "I never took anything from you that you weren't prepared to give."

"No? How about that last time?" she demanded, the hurt raw in her voice. "I certainly wasn't willing then."

His jaw tightened. "That was ... different."

"Yes," she agreed harshly. "Unforgettably different!"

There was a short tense silence that Nick broke by saying heavily, "It isn't over between us, Holly.

Not yet. Too much has been left unsaid, too many old wounds opened up for us just to walk away from one another." He paused, then added deliberately, "And you know as well as I do that before we're through we're going to make love again... *and it's going to be soon*. That, too, is still between us." He bent to pick up her stole and tossed it onto the bed. For a moment he looked at her, but when she didn't speak, said mockingly, "Sweet dreams, Holly," and left the room, shutting the door softly behind him.

CHAPTER SIX

FELIX RIDDELL'S YACHT, the *Alexis*, captained by the same man who had brought her the message the previous evening, picked Holly up punctually at ten the next morning, and took her over a sea as calm as glass across to Fallipos. At the jetty she was met by an austere English butler who conducted her—led was hardly the appropriate word—to where Felix Riddell waited for her in the large room that overlooked the garden.

He moved forward to greet her as soon as she came in, a lazy smile on his handsome face. "Good morning, Holly. I trust you've now fully recovered from your unfortunate dip in the sea?"

She smiled. "Yes, thank you. I'm fine." She held out the parcel of clothes she had borrowed. "And thank you for lending me these clothes, Mr. Riddell."

He waved the parcel aside. "I believe I told you to keep them. And the name's Felix." Putting a hand under her elbow, he led her to the long settee and poured her out a martini without bothering to ask her what she'd like, then he sat down beside her, one arm along the back of the seat. His eyes ran over her critically, as if he was summing her up all over again, but Holly returned his regard steadily, in no way intimidated. He smiled, his eyes crinkling up at the corners. "Tell me," he said lightly, "are we likely to have that husband of yours charging in on us again today?"

She shook her head, aware of the warning behind the question. "I hardly think so," she answered coolly.

"Good." He stood up. "How would you like to see my picture gallery?"

Holly's eyes widened a little in surprise; Felix Riddell was rumored to have an art collection that rivaled that of the late Paul Getty, including the most comprehensive set of French Impressionist paintings in the world. But he was like a miser with his hoard, never lending any of his paintings to exhibitions or allowing connoisseurs or other collectors to study or photograph them; many of his friends hadn't even been invited to look at them. So Holly felt more than a little overwhelmed by the unexpected privilege, then thought sardonically that perhaps he had a secondary collection that he allowed his visitors to see.

But in this she was mistaken; his gallery was like a massive walk-in safety vault with huge steel doors at the entrance, the paintings hung on bare white walls and lighted by electric light. The rich colors of Cezannes, Van Goghs, Gauguins and many others leaped at her in the long, stark room, overwhelming her at first by their sheer number and magnificence, but gradually, as she looked back down the gallery, she felt an infinite sadness that the power and beauty of the paintings should be shut away like this, hoarded for one man's pleasure.

Felix had led her slowly along, speaking knowledgeably of the paintings and their artists, and at first she had asked excited, eager questions, but as she grew silent he glanced at her with a puzzled frown.

"Doesn't art interest you?" he asked her abruptly.

"Yes, very much. I used to spend hours in art galleries in London when I was living in digs; they were the only places where you could go and get warm for nothing," she added with a reminiscent smile.

"But you don't like these pictures?"

Holly gave a slight frown and answered slowly, "Of course I like them, they're wonderful paintings, but .... I'm sorry, I don't mean to offend you, but I can't help thinking that so much beauty ought not to be shut away—they ought to be shared so that everyone can see them. I'm sure the artists never intended them to be locked away like this."

"Do you have any idea of the value of this collection?" he demanded.

She shook her head. "I'd hate to even make a guess. But surely—" she paused and looked at him uncertainly "—if a picture is taken out of circulation, then its value can only be judged by the amount of time you spend looking at it? Today you've spent about two minutes or so in front of each painting, but you probably spent ten minutes reading a newspaper, so the newspaper is worth five times as much to you as a painting."

Felix Riddell stared at her for a moment and then burst out laughing. "That is the most upside-down philosophy I've ever heard. But I must say it's original, I'll give you that." He glanced back down the gallery. "I suppose you're one of those people who think that all great paintings should be in public galleries; but has it never occurred to you that a painting won't last indefinitely, that it has to be kept in ideal conditions to preserve it as long as possible? And what better way to spend one's money than in trying to save as many of these great works as one can. Only the other day the Italian police recovered some paintings that had been stolen from a small gallery some months before, but the thieves had stored them in an old shed where they had been pecked at by chickens and soaked by rain and snow, so that they were all ruined beyond repair. At least I know that something similar will never happen to these while they're in my keeping."

Holly laughed lightly and held up her hands in surrender. "Okay, okay, I admit that there are two sides to every coin, but I still can't agree that they should be shut away like this."

Felix, too, laughed, an appreciative twinkle in his eyes, but continued to argue with her over the subject in a friendly way as he showed her out of the gallery and clanged the great steel doors shut behind them, sealing them by setting the buttons of an electronic gadget set in the wall.

"The locks are linked to a programmer in the computer room upstairs," he explained. "No one can open them without my orders."

He then took her over the rest of the house, acting rather like a guide in a showplace as he pointed out the pieces of sculpture and other objets d'art in the various rooms. For a few fleeting moments it seemed to Holly as if he was setting out to impress her with his wealth, although why he should want to she couldn't think. But he certainly seemed to be going out of his way to entertain a relatively unknown journalist who had intruded into his privacy. Holly looked at him with a puzzled frown between her brows, wondering if he just enjoyed showing off his possessions or whether he had some other motive in pointing them out to her. But then she shrugged the thought away; what other reason *could* there possibly be?

They had lunch out on the patio in the shade of a jasmine hedge, a wonderful meal that was a mixture of the most delicious Greek and French food. During the meal Felix put himself out to amuse her, making her laugh with anecdotes from his past about the rich and the famous people he had met. He was a witty and clever raconteur, knowing exactly how much detail to put into his stories and the precise moment for the punch line, so that Holly enjoyed herself immensely, tears of laughter in her eyes.

"Oh, no!" she gasped at one of his more way-out anecdotes. "He didn't do *that*? Not the *president*?"

But Felix assured her that it was true. "But don't spread it around or I might never get invited on his yacht again," he added with a grin.

Holly sat back and gently swirled the glass of Napoleon brandy he had poured for her. "Would that disappoint you very much?"

It was the first time she had asked him a personal question, but so far he had made no mention of giving her an interview for her paper and she was eager now to know where she stood, so she tried this as a tentative lead-in.

But Felix merely smiled and answered, "Not too much, no." He poured brandy from the crystal decanter into his own balloon glass and raised it to her in a silent toast. "But I've been talking too much. How about telling me something about yourself?"

"But I told you all about my career at breakfast yesterday."

"You also told me that you hadn't any commitments," he pointed out wryly, "and ten minutes later your husband showed up." He waited for her to speak, but when she didn't, he said softly, "Was he the one, Holly? The one who took the romance out of your life?"

She looked down at the table. "Something like that," she agreed, trying to keep her voice as even as she could.

Felix watched her keenly. "So what is it between you two? Are you separated, divorced or what?"

"I suppose you'd call it separated, although we've never consulted lawyers to make it legal or anything," she told him reluctantly.

He frowned. "So why is he with you now?"

Holly raised her head. "Look, do we have to go into this? I'm sure that my marriage can be of no earthly interest to you, so I'd rather just drop the whole subject, if you don't mind," she said shortly.

"But I *do* mind." His tone was so forceful that Holly's eyes widened in surprise. Setting down his glass, he leaned forward, his eyes regarding her steadily. "I want to know what your position is regard to your husband, Holly," he paused, then added deliberately, "and I want to know exacfly what your feelings are about him."

Holly blinked, taken aback by his sudden vehemence. Slowly she said, "He isn't with me. He was already here when I arrived, on a sailing holiday around the Greek islands. It was pure coincidence that he happened to be at Kinos when I came here to interview you."

"He didn't know you were coming?"

Shaking her head, she said decisively, "No, he couldn't have."

"When did you last see him, write to him? You may have mentioned it and forgotten about it."

She smiled wryly. "Oh, no. That's quite impossible. We haven't seen each other or communicated in any way for the last seven years."

"Seven years!" Felix stared at her in amazement. "But you must have been just a kid, then?"

"I was seventeen. As you say, just a kid," she agreed bitterly.

Felix's hand came out to cover hers. "What happened?" he asked gently.

She glanced quickly at him, a refusal to speak about her personal life again hovering on her lips, but there was such a kind, concerned look in his eyes that the words died unspoken.

His hand tightened on hers. "Tell me," he commanded.

"There's nothing to tell, really. We were both just too young—me especially. We lived with my parents, and they didn't get on with Nick. So he left...and forgot to take me with him. Absent-minded of him wasn't it?" she added with heavy irony.

Felix was watching her frowningly. "How long did it last?"

"About six months—give or take a few fights."

"I see." He sat back. "And I suppose seeing him here so unexpectedly has brought it all back, made the hurt raw again?"

Her hand trembled under his. "It has a bit, yes."

He grinned. "The British skill at understatement." Then he went on, "When is he moving on?"

Holly shrugged her shoulders and retrieved her hand. "I don't know. He seems to be sticking around." She didn't think that she had given anything away in her voice, but Felix looked at her shrewdly.

"Maybe he wants you back?"

"No, I'm sure that isn't his reason for . . . ." She broke off, a faint flush in her cheeks.

"So what is his reason?" Felix pursued. He looked at her face, then said thoughtfully, "Or maybe I can guess. He wants to go to bed with you again, is that it? Wants to satisfy his curiosity about what he saw in you in the past, about what kind of woman you are now."

"I would hardly think that he'll find that out just by sleeping with me again," Holly retorted acidly.

"That's where you're wrong." Felix leaned forward and picked up her hand again, easily overcoming her resistance, and holding it in both of his. "A man can find out everything he wants to know about a woman when he makes love to her. A woman has no secrets in bed." He paused, looking down at her hand and playing with her fingers, before saying almost casually, "Are you going to let him?"

Despite herself, her hand jerked in his. "That's none of your business," she returned coldly.

He lifted his head and looked at her steadily. "Maybe it's not ... but I'd very much like it to be," he added deliberately, his eyes holding hers.

Holly stared at him for a long moment. It was impossible to have misunderstood, impossible not to read the message in his eyes. In some confusion, she pulled her hand away and stood up. "If ... if you'll excuse me, I'll just go and freshen up."

"Of course."

He, too, stood up, and Holly could feel him watching her as she walked across the patio and entered the villa. Once in the cloakroom, she thankfully locked the door behind her, grateful for a little privacy in which to collect her thoughts. Slowly she crossed to the mirror over the marble sink and stared at her reflection in the glass. Her skin was quite tanned now, but even this healthy glow couldn't hide the dark smudges under her eyes, or the frown of worry in them. She hadn't slept much last night, even though she was tired, after that row with Nick. She had lain awake, thinking about him, her body still hot and frustrated from the way he had kissed her, caressed her. The thought of his fingers touching her made her toss and turn on the bed, longing for fulfillment. She wanted him to take her, she knew that, wanted it desperately after all these long empty years. For a while she had even been on the point of getting up and going to his boat, to wake him and tell him that she'd changed her mind, that she wanted to go to bed with him. But pride held her back. To go to him now would be utter weakness, almost as if she was saying that all the hurt and unhappiness he had caused her didn't matter. It would be a betrayal by her own body. So she had deliberately made herself remember the bad times in a feeble attempt to strengthen her resolve, a resolve she knew would be sorely tried the next time Nick tried to take her. And that there would be a next time, she had no doubt at all. He had said that he wanted her, and she knew him well enough to know that he would ruthlessly pursue that aim ... and what the end would be she was afraid to even begin to imagine.

She bent to wash her hands and sighed exhaustedly; this assignment was going completely wrong. First Nick had exploded onto the scene, and now Felix Riddell was causing complications. His last remark had made it perfectly clear that he was interested in her, which raised added problems, the most important being had he just invited her here for his own ends or did he really intend to give her an interview for her paper? Holly swore under her breath. Damn all men! She had managed to keep free of them for so long, and now they were threatening to disrupt her life again. Almost viciously she reapplied her lipstick and then strode back out to the terrace, in no mood for even the mildest flirtation, ready to snap Felix's head off if he tried it. In fact, she would almost have welcomed the chance, so that she could lose her temper, tell him just what

she thought of old men chasing young girls, so that
he would have nothing more to do with her and she
could pack up and go home, never to see either of
them again!

But Felix was more than her match when it came
to experience with women; he took one look at the
belligerent light in her eyes and kept the topics of
conversation completely impersonal for the rest of
the afternoon, so that gradually she relaxed and began to enjoy his company again. So much so that
once or twice she tried to steer him back to the
question of an interview, but he refused to commit
himself one way or the other, merely grinning and
changing the subject.

They went for a swim from the beach where she
had been washed up, then had a game of tennis
before changing for dinner, Holly again borrowing
a dress from the extensive wardrobe he kept for
female guests. She had been in two minds about
staying, uneasy about his intentions, but apart from
that one remark after lunch, Felix had made no attempt to make a pass at her, and when he saw her
hesitate, had smiled and said, "And of course my
yacht will be waiting to take you home whenever
you're ready." So they had dined by candlelight on
the richest, most wonderful food she had ever
tasted, served on dishes of the finest porcelain once
owned by the czars of Russia, and drank wine from
crystal glasses that reflected the light in a rainbow of
colors. Then they sat in the big lounge and listened
to music from equipment so sophisticated that the
orchestra seemed to be all around them. A log fire
took the chill off the evening, and Holly grew
sleepy and comfortable.

Felix came over to take her empty glass from her. "Another drink?"

She shook her head and straightened up from where she had been half lying on a settee. "No, I must go—it must be getting late." She glanced around and then remembered that he didn't have any clock in the room. "How do you tell the time when it's dark?"

He laughed. "Oh, I just go to bed when I feel tired and get up when I wake. But there's no reason why you shouldn't know the time." He crossed to his desk and took out a slim black box from the top drawer. He held it out to her. "Here."

Slowly she took the box from him and opened it. Inside was a watch on a slim gold band—real gold! After only a moment Holly shut the box again and handed it back to him. "I'm sorry, Felix, but I can't accept this."

He frowned. "Why not?"

"You know perfectly well why not." She stood up agitatedly. "I'll go and change."

"Holly." Felix reached out and caught her arm. "Don't read something into this gift that isn't there. It isn't even a gift, really—just a replacement for the watch you ruined when you went into the sea off my boat."

"It isn't necessary; I can get my own watch mended when I get home."

Rather exasperatedly he said, "That watch is made in one of my own factories; I keep a dozen of them here to give to friends."

"Maybe you do," Holly answered unsteadily. "Maybe an expensive gift like that is nothing to them, or to you. But it is to me ... *and you know it.*"

"All right." He looked at the heightened color in her cheeks for a long moment, then let her go. "All right," he repeated. "I'll tell them to have the boat ready to take you back to Melmia in twenty minutes."

He was waiting for her when she came down in her own clothes and took her elbow to guide her through the moonlit garden to the jetty. But just before they emerged from the trees he stopped and turned her to face him.

"Will you come again tomorrow?"

Holly hesitated, wondering if there was any point. Guessing the reason, Felix said earnestly, "Look, I know you still want the interview, but I haven't yet made up my mind. I'd like us to get to know each other better first. I need to be sure that you'd give me a sympathetic hearing before I commit myself."

There was a note of sincerity in his voice that enabled Holly to make up her mind. "All right, I'll come tomorrow." She held out her hand and smiled at him. "Thank you for a wonderful day."

He took her hand, but instead of shaking it carried it to his lips. "Good night, Holly."

It was late when the yacht pulled into the harbor at Melmia, but there were still a few men sitting on the terrace of the *taverna*, involved in one of the constant, unending arguments that were their greatest pleasure. As she hurried by, Holly glanced quickly up, half expecting to see Nick at one of the tables, but the men were all native Greeks. Then, as she climbed the outer stair, she saw him on the deck of his boat, leaning nonchalantly against the mast, smoking a cigarette. Quickly she turned and ran up the rest of the steps and dived into the corridor, hoping against hope that he hadn't seen her, but knowing full well that he had. In her room she hurriedly locked the door, then ran to the window. He was no longer on the deck and she couldn't see him on the street. Hardly able to breathe, she waited, expecting any second to hear his rap on the door, hear him demand that she let him in. But all was quiet and still, even the Greek men soon leaving. Slowly she relaxed and undressed, then went to close the shutters. Nick's boat was in darkness, like all the others in the harbor, swaying gently to the soft roll of the sea. She closed the shutters, closing Nick out, closing her mind to whether or not she would have opened the door to him if he had come to her room.

The yacht came for her at the same time and she again spent the day very pleasantly with Felix, learning to play squash in one of his two squash courts and after dinner watching a newly released American film in his private cinema. Again he had said no word about the interview and again he hadn't made a pass, although when he said good-night to her before putting her on the boat, he this time kissed her lightly on the lips. "Until tomorrow," he said softly.

Nick's boat was still tied up at the jetty, and he was again on deck smoking a last cigarette, but as he saw her disembark from the yacht, he threw the stub into the sea and went below. Almost as if he had been waiting up to see her safely home, Holly thought, feeling half resentful, half .... But what her other feelings were, she wasn't quite sure herself.

The next two days followed the same pattern with only a couple of phone calls from the features editor to disturb it. Holly had already told him that she was working on Riddell, but he was becoming impatient with her lack of progress.

"You don't understand the situation," she explained. "He's a tough nut to crack. If I try and push him he'll just tell me to go to hell. But I'm sure he will make up his mind before too long."

"Okay, stay with it. You've done fine to have gone so far," the editor assured her. "But try to clinch it as soon as you can, will you? If any other papers get wind of the likelihood of him telling his story, they'll all be there like a pack of wolves."

But it was the next day before Felix finally made up his mind. After dinner he led her to a room she hadn't been in before and which he described as his den. The walls were lined with shelves of books, many of them extremely early and valuable ones from their titles and cover bindings, although Holly was far from being an expert. He poured out a couple of drinks from a decanter on an antique sideboard and gave one to her.

"Let's drink a toast, shall we?"

Holly smiled. "By all means—but what to?"

He looked at her quizzically. "To you. To my new biographer."

She stared and then gulped. "I . . . I don't understand. You mean you want me to write your biography?"

He nodded, amused at her stunned expression.

"That's right. I've been thinking about it for the last few days, and I sent to London for examples of some of the work you've done in the past. Now that I've seen them I've decided to give you the job."

"So *that* was why you wouldn't make up your mind?" Her face glowed with excitement. "Oh, Felix, I'd love to do it. And I'll really do my best for you. You won't be sorry, I promise."

He laughed and put his arm around her waist. "I know I won't. I'm sure you'll do a great job."

She turned to him impulsively. "When can we start—tomorrow? I'll bring my cassette recorder and we can do enough for my newspaper article, and then I'll fly back to England and get leave of absence for a few weeks so that I can—"

"Hey, hold your horses," Felix interrupted her. "I said a biography; I didn't mention the newspaper feature."

Holly stared at him blankly, the excitement gradually leaving her face. "But I have to do that. I can't just forget about it and do your biography—it wouldn't be right."

"Well, right or not, that's the way it has to be," he said brusquely. "And besides, printing an article beforehand would steal a great deal of thunder from the biography, wouldn't it?"

"It might, yes, but...." Holly thought quickly. "Look, if you don't want the article written, would you agree to let my paper serialize your biography just prior to publication? That's been done many times before without harming the sales—in fact it quite often boosts them."

Felix rubbed his chin thoughtfully. "Okay, I'll buy that. Yes, we'll negotiate a deal with them straightaway."

Holly laughed happily. "That's wonderful. Oh, Felix, I'm eternally grateful. I'll fly over tomorrow and arrange it."

Felix put his other hand on her waist. "That won't be necessary; we can get in touch with them through my telex system. And besides—" he smiled down at her "—I don't want to lose you, even for a day." And drawing her to him, he bent his head to kiss her. He must have felt Holly stiffen but he went on kissing her, not letting her go for some time. Then she stepped back and looked at him bleakly.

"Just what are you trying to say?"

"You know perfectly well," he answered thickly. "I want you to stay here and live with me, Holly."

"Be your mistress, you mean?" she said coldly.

He reached out and again pulled her close. "We'd be *lovers*, Holly. You must know how I feel about you. I never thought I'd fall for anyone again, but I've fallen for you more heavily than any woman before. I want to—"

"Stop it!" Holly jerked away from him, her face white. "You're wasting your time." Agitatedly she took a few paces away from him as she tried to find the right words. "Felix, I'm sorry, but I don't feel the same way. So let's just drop the subject, shall we?"

Felix stared at her, a look almost of disbelief on his face. Then he said, "But we get on well together, don't we? You've enjoyed the days you've spent here with me?"

"Yes. Yes, of course I have, but—"

Stepping quickly across to her, he said, "Do you realize the kind of life I can give you, Holly? Anything and everything you want. Clothes, jewels. You'd have nothing but the best. We'd live here on the island together, just the two of us, but if you wanted to we could travel, go wherever you like. And I'd be generous, Holly. You wouldn't have to work ever again. No more running around the world chasing stories or living in cheap hotel rooms."

Holly had been vainly trying to interrupt and at last she managed to stop him. "But I *like* the life I live, can't you see that? I've worked hard to get where I am and I enjoy my job. And to live off your wealth, to have everything handed to me on a golden plate—where's the challenge in that? Okay, so maybe you've lived your life, answered all the challenges and can sit back and take things easy, but I still have mine to live."

She paused and looked at him unhappily. "And there's nothing you can give me that I want. All right, so it was exciting for a while to live like a millionaire; to wear beautiful clothes and have a mink coat put around me against the chill on an evening stroll, to be waited on and spend all the day in idle pleasure. But it was only exciting because I knew it would soon end, because I'd soon be back in my own world. If I lived like that all the time, never working, I'd be bored to death in weeks. The island would become a prison."

She moved to leave the room, but Felix caught her arm and turned her to face him. His voice was sharper now, with an edge of anger to it. "No. You

wouldn't be bored, Holly. Do you think me so inexperienced a lover that I wouldn't make you happy
and contented? Once we'd slept together you'd
want to stay with me for always."

He tried to take her in his arms again but she
pushed him away, her face set. "I'm sorry, Felix,
but the answer's still no. There's nothing you can
give me that I don't already have."

His mouth setting into a thin line, Felix said
harshly, "You don't have a man."

Holly's face paled. "I don't need a man. Not you,
or anyone," she retorted. Quickly she crossed to
the door. "Don't bother to see me out. I'll make
my own way to the boat."

His voice stopped her as she was about to leave.
"Do you know what you're giving up?"

She glanced back, a bitter smile on her lips. "Oh,
yes, I know that very well. I'm giving up every
chance of writing not only your biography but the
article as well."

"That isn't so." Holly had turned away, but his
words made her look back over her shoulder in surprise. "Your acceptance or refusal to my ... offer
had nothing to do with that. I'll give you the interview if you still want it. But the biography—" he
shrugged "—perhaps it would be better if we forgot
about that, in the circumstances. Being alone with
you for weeks on end, on a purely business basis,
might be more than I could stand."

Slowly Holly turned back into the room. "You ...
you mean it? You'll give me the interview ... and
with no strings?"

He smiled crookedly. "No strings. Come as usual

tomorrow, and bring your cassette recorder."
Then, brusquely, "You'd better go now. I'll tell
them to have the yacht ready for you."

It was almost midnight when the boat dropped
her at Melmia harbor and turned to go back to Fallipos. Holly watched it for a few minutes before letting her eyes look in the direction of Nick's boat,
drawn there as if from the pull of a powerful magnet. He wasn't on deck, but there was the glow of
light behind the curtains screening the cabin windows. And really there was no need for him to look
out for her. He must have realized by now that he
had only to hear the noise of the yacht's powerful
engines entering the harbor to know that she was
safely back.

Slowly Holly climbed the stairs to her room, her
thoughts in some confusion. Her rejection of Felix's proposition had been purely instinctive. She
had even found it a little repulsive, although why
she did so she wasn't quite sure. It certainly wasn't
because she found him physically repellent; even
though he was almost old enough to be her father
he was still a very handsome man and he had a
youthful outlook that easily bridged the age gap between them. He had touched her often and when
he had kissed her it hadn't been unpleasant. In fact,
Felix was a very experienced man who knew how
to handle women and how to make himself attractive to them. So why, then, had she found the
thought of becoming his mistress so repugnant?
Crossing to the window, Holly leaned on the ledge
and looked out, turning the problem over in her
mind until she came to the conclusion that it was

because Felix found it necessary to set out to make himself attractive that she had been put off. It suggested a degree of falseness in his character, and how could you ever rely on or trust someone who didn't act completely naturally with you?

She smiled slightly to herself, remembering the inducements he had offered her. How little he knew her character if he thought that clothes and jewels could influence her decision. How much more satisfying it was to see in print an article that you'd gone to endless lengths to obtain, had sweated and slaved over to get the wording exactly right. Okay, she had enjoyed their conversations together, had been stimulated and amused by him. He was the sort of person she would like to have as a friend, to meet, have dinner and laugh with occasionally. But he wasn't the sort of person she felt she could go to in trouble, or to confide in. Why, she hadn't even told him about Jamie.

But then she hadn't told Nick about Jamie, either. She came out of her reverie a little and realized that she had been gazing down at Nick's boat the whole time. It was getting quite late and yet the light still burned in his cabin; perhaps he was reading before he settled down to sleep. That was one of the things they had shared—a love of books. Almost every night they had been together they had read in bed for a while, until Nick had reached over and taken the book from her hands and pulled her down beside him. Holly's eyes filled with sudden tears, and she blinked them angrily away. Nick had never had to put on an act to make himself attractive. He possessed an arrant masculinity that made women physically aware and drew them to him like a magnet. And she had been so proud, so over the moon with joy when, of all the girls who had wanted him, he had chosen her. And Nick wasn't the promiscuous type; even after their marriage other women had made advances to him, had made it plain that they were available, but Nick hadn't even given them a glance, had only laughed at her fears and petty jealousies and told her that he was a one-woman man, and then had taken her in his arms and convinced her in no uncertain terms that she was definitely that one woman.

But now? She had sensed right from the start that he was different, far more widely experienced with her sex. There was a hardness about him that had never been there before, as if he really didn't give a damn. And the way he had kissed her, that, too, had shown her that there had been other women in his life, loving him, sharing his bed!

Holly straightened up suddenly, and without giving herself time to think about what she was doing, picked up her stole and ran out of the room and down the outside stairs. The moon was high in the night sky, casting a silver glow over the sleeping town, the walls of the cubelike houses creating sharp triangles of deep shadow at every corner. The terrace of the *taverna* was empty, although there was still a glow of light from the doorway leading to the kitchen where Alexis Lambis and his family would be having their own belated supper now that all the customers had gone home. Holly hurried on down the quay, not really knowing why she was going to Nick, or what she would say when she got there, just knowing that she *had* to see him.

Her heart beating painfully in her chest, Holly paused for a moment on the quay just above Nick's boat to recover her breath and try to compose herself a little. But as she stood there one half of the double doors leading to the cabin opened and the light spilled out onto the deck. She drew back, startled, then thought that Nick must have seen her and be coming to help her aboard. But the voice that came from the cabin definitely wasn't Nick's. It had a French accent and was feminine and husky.

"Oh, Nicholas, *mon chéri*, that was wonderful, *ravissant.*"

Holly hastily stepped back into a block of shadow and drew her dark stole over her light-colored dress as the doors opened fully and Chantel D'Anneau stood in the doorway and turned to put her arms around Nick's neck and kiss him on the mouth, her body pressed against his. *"A demain, chéri,"* she murmured throatily, and went on to say something else, but Holly didn't stay around to hear. She stepped farther into the shadow and slipped down the alleyway between two houses, running quietly along an inner path that she knew would take her back to the *taverna* and the sanctuary of her room.

CHAPTER SEVEN

HOLLY LAY AWAKE for most of that night, alternately cursing herself for being a stupid fool, or thanking her stars that she hadn't gone to Nick's boat earlier and walked in on him with the Frenchwoman. She shuddered at the thought, imagining the scene. She had acted purely on impulse, for once letting her heart rule her head, and look where it had got her! By running to him like that she had lowered herself to Chantel D'Anneau's level. She wondered whether the Frenchwoman's husband knew that she was visiting Nick on his boat at night, and, if not, how on earth the woman managed to sneak away and back again without being seen or missed. But perhaps the poor man was used to his wife's promiscuous behavior, Holly thought cynically, and either turned a blind eye or complacently accepted it. For all she knew it might be the accepted thing among the rich set they obviously belonged to, to have casual holiday affairs. And had Nick really sunk that low, that he'd let himself be used like that?

Holly turned to bury her head in her pillow, trying to shut out the pictures that filled her mind, but for the first time in years she cried herself to sleep.

Felix sent his yacht for her as usual the next

morning, but Holly was late and kept it waiting at anchor for several minutes, and when she did go aboard went straight inside to the cabin, her eyes hidden by dark glasses. There was a constraint between Felix and Holly today that she didn't even try to dispel. She got down to business right away, asking him questions from the long list she had prepared when she first came out to Kinos, which seemed aeons ago now. Felix answered readily enough, often making lengthy answers when she asked him to fill out his replies, but there was a frown between his brows as he watched her and noted her tenseness. At lunchtime he called a halt and insisted they talk of other topics over their meal, whereas Holly would rather have gone on with the interview. All she wanted now was to get enough information for her article and to go home to her son. She ate very little and answered him only in monosyllables, impatient to get on. But Felix seemed in no hurry now, although at first he, too, appeared to want to get the interview over. Holly had expected that, had been sure that her rejection of him would have made him at least brusque with her, if not downright nasty. To most men, expecially of Felix's age, the physical refusal of their advances by a young girl must come as a double blow, not only to their pride but to their vanity, highlighting the fact that they are no longer an attractive proposition. But for some reason she couldn't fathom, Felix seemed to want to get back on their old footing. Ordinarily Holly would have been pleased and happy to do so, glad to have him just as a friend, but she began to suspect that Felix might have thought she was just playing hard to get. Perhaps he was working up to asking her again, so she decided to keep it cool and by her manner let him know in no uncertain terms that she wasn't interested.

After lunch they started again, sitting outside on the patio, but Holly developed a blinding headache and found it almost impossible to concentrate. She asked the same question twice, apologized stumblingly, and put her hand up yet again to her aching head.

Felix stood up abruptly and crossing to her chair, firmly took her notebook from her hand and switched off the tape recorder. Holly opened her mouth to protest, but stopped as he took off her dark glasses and looked down grimly at her eyes, dark shadowed and still slightly puffy from the previous night. His mouth tightened.

"You've been crying."

Holly started to shake her head in denial, then realized the futility of it. "It's nothing to do with what happened between us last night, if that's what you're thinking. Let's get on, shall we? I'm not even halfway through yet."

She held out her hand for her glasses and after a moment he gave them to her, but said, "No, we've done enough for today. You don't look at all well."

"I have a headache, that's all," Holly admitted defensively. "If you could just ask someone to find me a couple of aspirins, I'll be fine shortly."

"No, we'll leave it now and carry on tomorrow, if you feel up to it. Let's go inside, out of the sun." He led her indoors and poured her an iced drink.

Then he left her a few minutes to come back with a bottle of painkillers. "Here, take a couple of these." He poured two into her hand and watched her as she swallowed them. "You young idiot, why didn't you tell me earlier that you weren't feeling well?"

"I...I wanted to get the interview over." She turned and went to sit on a settee, leaning her head back against the seat and shutting her eyes for a few blissful moments. When she opened them she saw Felix looking down at her, concern in his face.

"Why don't you go upstairs and lie down for a while?"

She managed a weak smile. "I'm sure it will go away soon. I'm sorry to be such a nuisance."

"My dear child!" Felix ejaculated, then bit off what he had been going to add and crossed to pour himself a drink, turning afterward to study her again. "You say it wasn't our—" he sought for a safe description "—our...disagreement last night that upset you? Is that the truth?"

Holly gave a rueful smile. "It didn't help any, but it wasn't the main cause, no."

"What was it, then?"

She looked away before saying shortly, "It really isn't any concern of yours, Felix."

"Which means that it was that husband of yours who made you cry," he guessed, a wry twist to his lips. "What did he do—try to force himself on you again?"

Holly stood up and faced him coldly. "No. *Yours* was the only proposition I received yesterday. As a matter of fact, I haven't even spoken to him for several days. And now, if you don't mind, I think

I'd like to be taken back to my hotel. I'm sorry about having to cut short the interview—I'm sure you're as keen as I am to get it over with as soon as possible."

"Holly, look, about last night...." Felix came over to her and reached out as if to take hold of her arms, but she moved away.

"It's all right, you don't have to say anything." She lifted an unsteady hand to her head. "I'm afraid I was rather rude to you, and I'm sorry."

"Hell, no. I should be the one to apologize." Felix appeared as if he was going to say something else, but looked at her white face and changed his mind. "We'll talk when you're feeling better. Phone me from the hotel tomorrow if you feel up to it, and I'll send the boat for you."

"Yes, all right," Holly agreed tonelessly, and allowed him to escort her down to the quay and help her onto the yacht.

By the time they got back to Melmia the painkillers had helped a lot, but she still felt very tired, so she decided to go for a quick swim and then relax on the beach for a while. There were different people on the sands today, the ferry having brought a new set of holidaymakers. A couple of young men looked her over appreciatively as she passed, but she ignored their attempts to talk to her and walked farther up the shore, looking for a quiet spot away from everyone else. She found it where two largish rocks jutted out from the beach forming a roofless cave with a stretch of pure, clear sand a few yards wide between them.

Holly didn't swim for very long, just enough to

cool herself off, then she retreated to her patch of
beach and lay down on her towel, her head in the
shadow cast by one of the rocks, the rest of her
body in the sun. She tried to go to sleep, but it
eluded her. Her mind was still too full of Nick and
the Frenchwoman. There had been no sign of her
or any of her friends on the beach today, and their
boat hadn't been in the harbor, so presumably they
had gone sailing for the day... unless they had left
Kinos altogether. Was that what it had been last
night, Holly wondered; a farewell fling before
Chantel D'Anneau and her party moved on? Or
had she been heard going back to her boat so that
her husband found her out and decided to remove
her from Nick's dangerous proximity? It would be
interesting to see whether or not their boat came
back that evening.

Turning onto her stomach, Holly let the soft
sand drift through her fingers. Perhaps Nick was so
smitten with the Frenchwoman that he might also
sail away, follow them to wherever they were
headed. But this new, harder Nick didn't seem as if
he would ever let a woman get close enough to him
to upset his plans in any way. If they couldn't fit in
with him it was just too bad. A "so long, it was fun
while it lasted" attitude. Not that Holly cared either
way, of course; it meant nothing to her how many
women Nick had, now or in the past. She stared at
the fine sand flowing gently from her hand; so why,
then, had she cried last night? For the old Nick, for
the one who had never looked at another woman
when he was with her? Or was it guilt, because it
was her fault that he had become the man he now

was? She had been so blind then, so terribly blind.

Abruptly she got up. This self-recrimination just wouldn't do. She knew from past experience that it only made things worse, eating away at her shaky confidence and making her more open than ever to hurt and unhappiness. She had found then, when Nick went away, that action was the only answer, so now she ran down the beach and plunged into the sea again, swimming out strongly against the swell.

The two youths must have seen her, for they, too, swam out and caught up to her as she turned back. They spoke to her first in a language she didn't understand, and she shook her head as she tried to swim away from them. But they came after her and one said in bad English, "You in trouble. We help, yes?" He caught hold of her arm.

"No. I'm all right." Holly tried to protest but the second youth grabbed her other arm.

They were in shallower water now and the two men could stand up, although Holly was still floating. They were laughing at her, leering grins on their faces, as their free hands began to explore her body. Holly opened her mouth to scream but they pulled her under so that she choked and gasped on swallowed water.

"You like this game, yes?" One of the youths, his dark hair plastered to his head, laughed in her face as his hand started to pull off the bottom half of her bikini.

The next moment he disappeared beneath the surface, his hand torn from its grasp on her arm. There was a froth of struggling arms and legs and

Holly's eyes opened in amazement as Nick's head broke the surface, her assailant hanging limply from the arm lock in which Nick held him. The other youth, too, was gaping in astonishment, and then he hastily let go of her and plunged away, heading for the other end of the beach as fast as he could swim.

"Are you all right?" Nick seemed hardly even out of breath.

"Y-yes, thanks." Holly reached down and wriggled back into her bikini. "What are you going to do with him?" She nodded toward the half-dazed youth.

"I know what I'd like to do with him," Nick said grimly, "but I suppose we'll have to let him go."

He half carried, half dragged him nearer the beach and then loosened his hold so that the youth fell to his knees in the water, then got up and staggered away in terror, constantly looking back in case Nick was coming after him.

When he'd gone, Nick turned to look at Holly, putting out a gentle finger to touch the red marks on her arm where they'd held her. "Did they hurt you very much?"

"No." Holly shook her head, but then trembled. "But it wasn't ... very pleasant." She walked out of the water and back up the beach and bent to pick up her towel. "I felt so *helpless*."

Nick took the towel from her and wrapped it around her shoulders, then began to rub her back. "You need some lessons in self-defense."

"Yes," Holly agreed with a certain amount of irony in her voice. "I suppose I do."

Nick caught the implication and his hands stilled as he looked down into her face for a long moment. Then he said abruptly, "You're back early today. What happened—did you have a row with your millionaire?"

"No, I didn't...and he isn't *my* millionaire," Holly pointed out, her tone hardening.

"No?" Nick's left eyebrow rose in disbelief. "You surely aren't going to tell me that it takes as long as this to get the facts for one article?"

"Of course it doesn't."

"So just what have you two been doing for the last week—playing chess?" he asked, his lips twisting into a sarcastic sneer.

"Yes...among other things, if you must know," Holly returned, angry now. "Not that's it's any of your damned business what I do with my time."

Nick's eyes blazed. "And I suppose it's none of my damned business who my wife gives her body to, either?"

"No, it isn't," Holly began furiously, "because I don't consider myself to be your wife. In fact, I—"

Even through the thickness of the towel, Holly could feel his grip tighten on her shoulders. "Have you been to bed with him yet? Have you?" he demanded savagely.

"What's the matter?" Holly jeered. "Are you jealous because I prefer him to you? Well, you're right to be, because he's a far better lover than you ever were! He's twice the man you—" She stopped abruptly, the words choked off as Nick put his hand to her throat, his eyes murderous in his set face.

"Is he, by God?" His expression changed. "Or is

the attraction just the obvious one that he's rolling in money? Is that why you let him proposition you—for what you could get out of him?" he sneered.

Holly knocked his hand away and stepped back. "Well, whatever I see in Felix, it's perfectly obvious what you see in Chantel D'Anneau," she retorted fiercely.

Nick's eyes fastened on her face. "Just what is that supposed to mean?"

"It means what the hell right have you to question me when you're in the middle of a sordid affair with another woman yourself?"

A guarded look came into his face. "What gives you that impression?"

"Oh, it isn't an impression," Holly shot back caustically, "it's a fact. I saw her leaving your boat last night."

His eyebrows flew up in astonishment. "You *saw* her?"

"Yes, kissing you good-night and thanking you for the wonderful time you'd given her," she answered, her voice as cutting as a razor's edge.

Something flickered in his face and there was amusement in his voice as he said, "Well, at least I have one satisfied customer who's willing to give me a reference."

"Why, you!" Holly's voice shook with rage. She raised her arm to hit him, but Nick caught her wrist and held it.

"Holly, listen, there's nothing between—"

"No, you listen," Holly put in, her voice vitriolic. "When I met you again I was filled with all sorts of doubts and uncertainties, but this past week has taught me a lot. And I'm perfectly certain of one thing more than anything else; that I want to be free of you. Free forever. As soon as I get back to London I'm going to sue for a divorce!''

Nick's grip tightened on her wrist for a moment, but then it eased and he let go, his expression unreadable. "I see. And just when do you intend going back to London?"

Holly took a couple of deep breaths, trying to calm herself. Her nerves were in a sudden vacuum now that the decision had been taken, the words said. Her voice surprisingly steady, she answered, "I'm not sure. Probably the day after tomorrow."

"There isn't a ferry that day."

"It doesn't matter. I'll hire a boat to take me to Piraeus, and then I can get a plane from Athens."

"Perhaps you'll look me up before you go," Nick said flatly, "so that I can give you the address of my lawyer. You'll need it for the divorce," he added pointedly when he saw the wary look in her eyes. "And maybe you're right, maybe it would be best this way. After all, we don't have anything to hold us together."

"No." Holly turned away, unwilling to meet his eyes and unable to find anything else to say.

After a moment, Nick said heavily, "If you're ready to go I'll walk you back to the *taverna*. Those two chaps seem to have disappeared, but I'd rather you didn't go back alone."

Holly slipped her sundress over her head and bent to put on her flip-flops. "I haven't thanked you for coming to my rescue," she said stiffly.

"Think nothing of it, it's all part of the service," he answered with flippant irony.

But there was no sign of the youths, and Nick left

her at the edge of the town with a mere curt nod of farewell, and strode off down one of the side streets, leaving her to make her own way to the *taverna*. Now that the die was cast, Holly felt a curious sense of unreality and relief from tension. It was as if the bond holding them together had suddenly snapped, and she was left dangling in midair, at the end of one part of her life but not yet having started on the next. For the first time she was glad that she had seen him again, that things had come to a head, and the decision she had been putting off for years, finally made. But there was sadness there, too, and a sense of desolation and failure. Because that was all divorce could ever be, an admission of failure to make good from a bright and wonderful beginning.

The next morning she phoned Felix and asked him to send the yacht for her, determined to get the interview finished that day. With this in view, she kept strictly to business, refusing to let Felix sidetrack her. Over lunch he tried to lead her into more personal conversation, but Holly was politely distant, ready to talk on general topics but steering well clear of anything that might edge onto her private life. Felix looked at her in some bafflement, unable to get by the defensive wall Holly had thrown up between them.

In the afternoon they finished the interview and then he agreed to let her take photographs, and she used up several rolls of film on both him and the house. When she'd finished and was about to pack her camera back in the case, Felix stopped her.

"Lend me your camera; I want to take one of you."

Reluctantly she handed it over and Felix made her stand against a background of flowers in the garden, the oleander and jasmine filling her nostrils with their heady scents. Without thinking she reached up to a branch above her head and pulled it down, the better to smell the heavenly perfume. She felt a sudden sadness, knowing that she would never see this lovely place again, and closed her eyes for a moment, trying to imprison its beauty in her memory.

"Holly."

She opened her eyes to find Felix staring at her. There was an almost desperate appeal in his eyes as he quickly crossed to her, the camera forgotten, and gripped her arms. "Holly, don't go. I need you so much. Can't you see what you mean to me? Please say you'll stay."

"Felix, no, please." Holly tried to disengage herself, but he was holding her too tightly. "We've already been into all this. I don't want to be just your mistress...."

"And this time I'm not asking you to be." A rueful smile came to his lips. "After the last time I swore I'd never do this again, but if it's the only way to keep you with me .... I want you to marry me, Holly, to be my wife. I'm not going to lose you now, not after having found you. I never thought I'd fall in love again, but I have, harder than ever before. And you'll be my last love, Holly, I swear it."

He bent to kiss her, taking her acceptance for granted, his lips already possessive. When at last he let her go, Holly moved away, unhappiness in her eyes. During the course of that long interview she had learned the real reason for Felix's settling in Fallipos and cutting himself off completely from his former life. He'd said, "I simply woke up one morning with the most colossal hangover, my whole body feeling foul from too much food and drink, and too many cigarettes. And I didn't know where I was ... or a thing about the woman I was in bed with. It was then I realized that I was rapidly killing myself, and that the only way to stop was to get myself as far away from temptation as possible. At first I thought of shutting myself away in one of those monasteries where you can go as a guest to rest and think, but you can imagine the sort of field day the press would have made out of that if they had got wind of it, so I decided to play the eccentric millionaire and create this hideaway for myself. And I've grown to love it here, so much that I never want to leave it."

His confession had given her a much better understanding of him, and for a moment she almost wavered. It would be so easy to just opt out, to let Felix take over her life and Jamie's and never have any worries ever again, to live here in this peace and tranquillity. And Felix had said that he needed her. She felt an overwhelming surge of compassion for him and gratitude that he should want her so much. No one had ever told her they needed her before, not even Nick when they were together. But then she thought of Jamie, of his constant but unspoken need of her that was far greater than Felix's could ever be, and common sense reasserted itself. Felix had lived and played to excess before he came here, whereas she had only just begun to live, and Jamie not at all.

Her voice firm, she said, "I'm sorry, Felix, but I can't marry you."

"Because of your husband?" He dismissed her marriage with a wave of his hand. "You can file for a divorce immediately. You won't even have to leave here to do it. It can all be done for you by lawyers in London."

"No. It isn't that." As gently as she could, she said, "I don't love you, Felix. I like you very much, yes, and I'd be proud to have you as a friend. But I don't love you, and I can't live with someone I don't love."

A bleak, defeated look came into his eyes. "And what if I told you I couldn't live without you?"

Slowly she answered, "I'd say that you were too big a man to resort to that kind of blackmail. You lived without me before, Felix. You'll soon forget that I ever existed."

He shook his head. "No, that I'll never do."

Holly picked up her camera and Felix escorted her down to the quay, silently accepting his defeat, but before helping her onto the yacht he kissed her again, with a fierce, yearning hunger as if he couldn't bear to let her go. Then he said unevenly, "Maybe I've been here too long. Perhaps I'm ready to face the world again and strong enough to withstand all the excesses that brought me down before."

Reaching out to gently touch his cheek, Holly said with sincerity, "Oh, I hope so, Felix, I really do."

He let her go, then, and she stood in the stern of the boat as it pulled away, watching Felix and his island recede into the horizon and out of her life.

Back at Melmia, Holly hired a boat through Alexis Lambis. The fisherman owner agreed to leave early the next morning; then she phoned her office to tell them of her plans before going up to her room to pack her things. As she wanted to make an early start the next day, she changed into a black silk blouse and matching skirt and went down to the terrace to eat a couple of hours earlier than she would normally have done, intending to have an early night before the long journey ahead of her.

Then there was only one thing left to do. Holly walked slowly along the quay toward Nick's boat, the blood red of the setting sun lighting the sky on fire and turning the whitewashed houses to soft pink in its reflected glow. She walked past the spot where the French yacht had been moored, its place taken now by a converted fishing smack, and paused on the harbor wall by Nick's *Argosy*.

She supposed she ought to shout "Ahoy, there" or something to announce herself, but knew that she would feel ridiculous, so instead clambered down onto the boat and rapped on the cabin roof.

Almost immediately Nick pushed open the doors and stood on the steps, looking at her.

"You...you asked me to look you up before I left," Holly said when he didn't speak.

"Yes. Of course. Come in."

He went back down the steps and put up a hand to help her down, but she pretended not to see it and managed alone. The cabin was compactly fitted out with a galley on the right, opposite a dining section with a table now folded away and a row of seats down one side. Beyond, toward the bow, she could see into another cabin fitted with a wide bunk, neatly made up with pillows and a blanket. Holly took one glance, remembered Chantel D'Anneau and quickly looked away, her face set.

"Won't you sit down and have a drink?"

"Thanks, but I won't be staying. I only came because you said you'd give me the name of your lawyer," she answered stiffly.

"Of course. I'll write it down for you. And perhaps you'd better give me the address of yours."

Hastily Holly fished in her bag for paper and pen, and wrote it down for him. Then she turned to find that he was watching her. He glanced at the paper when she handed it to him, then slipped it into the pocket of the pale blue denims he was wearing.

"Afraid I'll have to search around a bit for mine. It's a firm that was recommended to me by someone in Australia. The card should be around somewhere, but it's easy to lose things in a small boat like this. In the meantime, we might as well have a drink. Yours was a vodka and tonic, wasn't it?" He opened a well-stocked liquor cabinet and poured out a vodka for her and Scotch for himself.

"Now, what will we drink to?" he asked as he handed her a glass. "I suppose the obvious thing would be to our future happiness."

"Apart," Holly added caustically before he lifted the glass to his lips.

He smiled crookedly. "As you say—apart."

Holly sat down on one of the seats because the cabin was so small that standing made her too close to Nick for comfort, while he leaned against the edge of the galley, making no move to search for the address.

After a couple of swallows, Holly reminded him tartly, "You said you were going to look for that card."

"There's plenty of time," he returned easily. "I take it your prolonged interview with Felix Riddell is now finished?"

"Yes," she agreed shortly, refusing to be drawn.

"So you'll be going back to London to write up your story. Any idea where they'll send you next?"

She shook her head. "It could be anywhere. But I hope to have some time at home first."

He raised his brows. "Home?"

"I have a cottage—" she paused "—in the country."

A quizzical look came into his eyes. "I hardly picture you in a country cottage with roses around the door. I would have thought an apartment in the West End of London was more in your line."

Holly set down her glass and stood up. "Well, you never did know me very well, did you? When you get around to finding that card, perhaps you'll send the address to my lawyers?"

Nick made no move to stop her as she left the cabin, merely following her up the steps to the cockpit. But then he said, "Before you go, perhaps you wouldn't mind giving me a hand for a minute? I've been having some trouble with my engine, and I'd like to try it out, make sure it's running properly."

Holly turned back reluctantly. "What do you want me to do?"

"Just steer the boat for a bit while I check that the engine is pumping the water through."

"You mean take it out to sea?" Holly asked uneasily. "Why can't you run it here?"

"I'd have to have the throttle wide open and it makes too much noise," Nick explained casually. "The sound of the engine reverberates on the dock wall, and also it creates too much wash; it would make all the boats move around when the owners are trying to cook their dinners, which wouldn't make me very popular. It won't take very long," he added, "and I'd prefer to get it right before it gets too dark."

"Oh, all right," Holly agreed reluctantly, long experience of old and reluctant car engines making her sympathetic to his difficulties. "What do you want me to do?"

"I'll take her out of the harbor, and then perhaps you could take over while I get down into the bilges."

He cast off the mooring lines and started the engine, to chug quietly out of the harbor, heading toward the sunset, the sea flecked with purple and gold in their wake. Once clear of the bay, Nick turned the boat to starboard, and Holly took over the wheel, sailing parallel with the shore. Automatically she obeyed Nick's instructions to accelerate or slow down, and then they sat idly on the water while he made some adjustments.

Holly had never been out to sea at sunset before, especially a Mediterranean sunset, and gradually she became lost in its magnificence, watching it slowly sink, glowing purple at the base of the orb and lightening to molten crimson above, shafts of blazing orange and gold reaching up into the deep blue of the sky. It was very quiet, the sea very still, as if the whole world had stopped and was breathlessly watching the miracle of transition from day into night. The sun sank lower, was suddenly blinding in its last brilliant intensity, and then it was gone, the heat and light and spirit lost from the day.

With a deep sigh, Holly slowly came back to reality to find Nick standing silently behind her, he, too, caught up in the beauty of the sunset. Its glow was still on his face, reflected in his eyes as he gazed down at her.

"I'll take over now."

Holly moved aside as he took the wheel and turned to watch the last dying rays as the boat came around. This, too, was a memory she wanted to hold on to and treasure, but she was filled with an inexpressible sadness, knowing that memory could never bring back the brilliance and beauty that she'd just seen.

Concentrating as she was on the last dying rays of the sunset, Holly didn't realize where they were until she heard the rattle of the anchor chain and looked around to see that Nick had sailed into a small deserted cove surrounded by steep cliffs that made it inaccessible except by sea. The anchor splashed down and the boat came broadside onto the shore, about thirty yards from the beach.

As Nick cut the engine, Holly turned to him questioningly. "What's the matter? Isn't the engine working properly?"

"Yes, it's fine." Deliberately he added, "It always was. I just wanted to get you alone."

Holly stared at him. "You tricked me into coming with you? Well, just what was the point?" she demanded angrily. "We've said everything there was to say and come to the only conclusion possible—that we never want to see each other again and intend to keep it that way—permanently."

"You're right," Nick agreed sardonically, "We *have* said everything we're going to say to one another for the time being. In fact we've already said too much ... and all of it the wrong things."

"Then why on earth ...?" Holly began hotly, then came to an abrupt stop as she saw the look on his face.

"Because we've some unfinished business, you and I."

"No!" The word came out in a gasp of fear, then hurriedly, "Look, if it's because of what I said about you and Felix—"

Nick laughed harshly. "Oh, no. This is nothing to do with Riddell or any other man there's been in your life. This is just between you and me."

"No!" Holly gasped again and made an involuntary movement to escape, but Nick reached out and caught her, pulling her to him, imprisoning her hands against his chest.

Roughly he said, "I've been trying to make you come to your senses since the moment we met, but it seems there's only one way to get through to you."

Terror in her voice, she stammered, "No, Nick, please. Please don't."

"It has to be this way." Picking her up, Nick kicked open the cabin door and carried her inside, then set her down on her feet. He took her arms and put them down at her side, then Holly stood as if turned to stone as he undid the fastening of her skirt and she felt it slip off her hips and fall to the deck. His fingers sought the buttons of her blouse, became impatient so that a button tore and clicked to the floor. He pulled off her blouse and let that, too, fall to the deck, then his hand moved to the fastening of her bra. She shuddered as his hands found the soft swell of her breasts, cool against his fingers. His lips touched her throat, murmuring her name, then went on down, caressing, urgent.

The memory of that last time, when he had taken her against her will and then left her, when he had given her a child, came forcibly back, filling her with fear, and she suddenly put her hands against his shoulders and pushed him violently away. Nick lost his balance and fell back, giving her time to turn and run for the door. She stumbled up the steps, sobbing with panic, running across to the rail and throwing herself into the sea as he burst out of the cabin after her.

The water was still warm from the sun, enfolding her like a blanket, but Holly paused only to kick off her sandals before striking out desperately for the shore, no clear idea of what she was going to do, intent only on getting away.

Behind her, Nick tore off his clothes and then dived cleanly from the deck, coming to the surface and breaking into a powerful crawl in one smooth, graceful movement. He caught her as she felt the bottom beneath her feet and began to run through the shallows, catching her arm and spinning her around. Holly fought him silently, kicking and clawing, tears running down her face because she knew it was a fight she couldn't win. She slipped on the wet sand and fell to the ground, Nick falling with her, their legs still in the lapping waves as they rolled over and over.

Suddenly Holly collapsed, letting him pinion her arms against the sand, his body heavy on top of her. They were both panting, breathless, and for a few moments lay inertly, then Nick's mouth sought hers, pushing her head back against the sand, forcing her mouth to open. Holly gave a little moan, trying to jerk her head away, but his lips continued to ravage hers, demanding submission. For a moment she continued to resist, but she could feel his body hard against her own, his thighs imprisoning hers. She moaned as her lips parted in the final surrender, her insides taking fire as Nick let go of her wrists to fondle and caress her. Then all other sensations deserted her as she lost herself in his embrace.

The water swirled and eddied around them as Nick reached down to pull off the rest of her clothes, then he made love to her in a frenzy of triumph and longing, their mutual ecstasy wild and prolonged. There was no night or day, no land or sea, only the two of them lost in a vortex of sensuality as old as time itself.

CHAPTER EIGHT

THE STARS WERE OUT and the first shafts of moonlight lit the sky when Nick at last stood up and
looked down at Holly lying at his feet. He stood tall
and strong as a tree, the drops of water running
down his thighs and legs. Holly looked up at him
sensuously, mouth parted, lids half closed, her face
softened by satiated rapture.

Nick smiled down at her, his eyes caressing her
nakedness. He bent to pick her up and Holly put
her arms around his neck, clinging to him and burying her head against his shoulder. Wading out into
the sea, he lay her on her back and swam with her
the last few yards, then hoisted her onto the boat,
before carrying her down to the cabin. He found a
big, soft towel and put it around her, intending to
dry her, but Holly reached up to twine her hands in
his hair, pulling his head down so that she could
kiss his throat, bite his ear.

"Behave yourself, woman." He tried to towel
her back but Holly moved closer to him, rubbing
herself sensuously against him until he groaned
deep in his throat. "You minx. Later I have to talk
to you."

"No, I don't want to talk." Holly ran her fingers

over his chest, touching, exploring, rediscovering her power over him.

He stood it for a little while, then let the towel drop so that he could hold her, kiss her with hungry passion. Then he led her into the forward cabin and gently laid her on the made-up berth, her fair hair falling across the pillows. For a moment he sat on the edge of the bunk, his eyes dark with desire as he fondled her.

Holly opened her arms to him. "I want you, Nick. I want you now."

He smiled, and as he came down on her he said forcefully, triumphantly, "You're my woman, Holly. You belong in my bed."

When Holly awoke she found the little cabin in darkness except for the glow of a cigarette as Nick lay smoking quietly beside her. He put it out when she stirred and put his arm around her, pillowing her head on his shoulder. Holly sighed contentedly and snuggled up to him. It had been so long, so very long since they had lain together like this.

Tenderly Nick pushed the hair off her face and stroked it gently as he said, "Holly, there's something I've got to tell you. I—"

She stiffened and interrupted fiercely, "If it's about that French tart—"

Nick laughed. "No, it isn't." He balled his hand into a fist and hit her playfully on the chin. "And I *wasn't* having an affair with her. If you'd hung around a minute longer you'd have seen her husband and another couple leave with her. I'd invited them over to the boat for supper and a drink in return for an invitation they'd given me. It was the food she'd enjoyed, not me, you jealous little cat."

Holly smiled in the darkness and nuzzled his neck, exploring it with little kisses. "I was, wasn't I? But she wanted you, though."

"Just like Felix Riddell wanted you," Nick reminded her gently.

She grew still and said with difficulty, "Nick, what I said about him—it wasn't true. I didn't go to bed with him."

"I know."

"You do?" Holly's eyes opened wide in surprise. "But how could you possibly know?"

He ran his fingers slowly down her arm so that she shivered deliciously. "A man can often tell when a woman hasn't been made love to for a long time—and you haven't, have you?"

"No," she whispered. "There hasn't been anyone since you."

"Oh, Holly. My darling girl." His hand tightened convulsively on her arm. "And Riddell? He didn't mean anything to you?"

"No." Holly shook her head.

Nick gave a sigh of relief. "If you knew the agonies of jealousy I went through seeing you go off in his boat every day. I wanted to tell you then how much I wanted you back, but everything seemed to be going wrong between us, and you'd built up such a wall around yourself, that I was afraid I'd only make things worse. If it hadn't been for the fact that you came home every night, I think I would have kidnapped you long since. And when I thought of you, possibly in his arms and making love to you, I wanted to go over there and tear him apart." He paused to explore her bare shoulder with his lips. "So I was wrong about him all the time," he murmured indistinctly. "It was just business?"

"Oh, I wouldn't say that," Holly answered casually, and smiled to herself when his head jerked up. "He *did* ask me to be his mistress."

"Oh, he did, did he? I hope you told him to go to hell?"

"No," Holly replied equably, "I said no, thank you, as a nicely brought-up girl should."

He laughed softly. "Minx. And I suppose that brought the interview to an abrupt end?"

"On the contrary, the interview didn't start until I'd turned him down."

His brows drawing into a frown, Nick said, "You mean that he used it as an inducement for you to accept?"

"No, there were no strings to either of his offers."

"Either...? He asked you again?"

"No. The second time he asked me to marry him," Holly replied calmly, mischievously enjoying his discomfiture.

"Did he, by God?" Nick sat up and stared down at her. "I trust you told him you were already married?" he said harshly.

"He didn't seem to think that was of much importance." A thunderous look came into Nick's eyes and he opened his mouth to make a biting retort, but Holly went on, "But I told him that I didn't love him, and that I could never give myself to a man I didn't love. Now or ever," she added softly.

Nick's expression changed immediately and he lay down again to gently trace the outline of her face with his fingers. "Oh, my lovely girl, if I could only tell you how much you mean to me." But he must have felt her stiffen, the hurt not yet completely gone, and he said urgently, "Listen to me, sweetheart. I didn't just walk out on you. I wrote to you at once telling you that I was going to look for a new job and somewhere for us to live. That I'd come for you as soon as I found somewhere. But when I telephoned a few days later, your mother said that you wanted nothing more to do with me, that everything was over between us. I came around to the house but your father said you'd gone to stay with friends and ordered me out. So then I spent ages traveling all over the country calling on all the friends and relatives I thought you might have gone to. During that time I'd applied for the job with the construction company again, and when I was sure I'd got it and knew where I was going, I went to your parents' house again and pushed my way in when they tried to keep me out. I ran up to our room, but it was empty, all your clothes gone. I went through the other rooms and then I tried to make them tell me where you were. I was angry, God how I was angry. I said some pretty foul things to them and they called the police and had me slung out." His voice filled with remembered bitterness. "It was then I came to the conclusion that what they had said was true—that you really didn't want to see me again."

Holly lay motionless beside him, realizing with growing horror how her parents had interfered to wreck her life even more than she'd known. When he'd finished she put her head in her hands and moaned. "Oh, no! No. Oh, Nick, I missed you so much and I was so alone. I wanted to die."

She began to cry, in sorrow for the years they had lost, for the terrible waste, as well as for the hurt that Nick must have suffered.

He let her cry for a little while, then gently lifted her head and kissed the tears away. "Hey, don't you want to hear the rest?"

Trying to control herself, Holly took a long, shuddering breath. "Yes. Yes, of course."

"Well, when I went away that first time I was pretty mad, but somehow I could never push you out of my mind or hate you, as I tried to do. I loved you very much, you see," he said simply. "So every time I came on leave to England I looked for you, but without any success. And then when I did find you, it was in Australia of all places."

"In Australia? But I don't understand; I've never been there."

Her eyes had grown accustomed to the darkness now and she saw him smile. "No, but a magazine with one of your articles in it, together with a small picture of you on the editorial page, found its way to the site where I was working. I immediately phoned your office, but they wouldn't give me your address, so I pretended that I might have a story for you, and they told me you were shortly coming here on another assignment."

Holly sat up and put on the light so that she could

see him properly. She stared down at him. "You knew I was coming to Kinos? It wasn't a coincidence?"

He grinned smugly. "Hardly. I caught the next plane and broke a couple of world records to get to Greece, and hire a boat, and sail out here before you arrived. I just made it; the ferry you were on sailed in a few hours after I did."

She was silent for a moment, going through the implications. "And did you come here hoping that we—that this might happen?" she asked slowly.

A serious look came into Nick's eyes. He reached up and gently began to massage her shoulders. "I'd like to say yes, but to be honest, I just didn't know. I only knew that I had to see you again, to hear from your own lips that we were finally through. We're two grown-up people now, not kids anymore, and maybe I thought we could meet and find out where and why we went wrong. Help us build for the future." He smiled wryly and his fingers tightened on her shoulders. "At least that's what I told myself, but I'm afraid that when I met you everything suddenly became far more basic than that."

"So I noticed." Holly lowered her head so that her hair fell forward and hid her face. She said, as lightly as she could, "Well, now you know that you can still make me. You've laid your ghosts and can start again as soon as you're free. We'll both be able to now that we don't have any feelings of guilt or bitterness about each other."

His hand lifted the curtain of her hair. "Is that what you want—to go ahead with the divorce?"

"Yes, of course. We've both built up different

lives for ourselves," Holly answered, trying to keep a light tone, but unable to meet his eyes.

Nick laughed softly and pulled her down to him. "Oh, Prickles, what a terrible liar you are." His lips found hers. "I love you," he murmured against her mouth. "I've never stopped loving you, and I'm never going to let you go again."

He made love to her again then, rediscovering a long-forgotten fire that had blazed and burned so long ago. It was different . . . and yet the same as she remembered. Love and gentleness were there now, as well as heat and passion. Bitterness disappeared as they gloried in each other's sensuality, lifted to dizzying heights of ecstasy that washed away all hurts and fears. And at last they lay in exhausted, contented sleep in each other's arms.

Holly woke first and sat up, careful not to disturb Nick who, even in his sleep, had placed a possessive arm across her waist. The light was still on and she reached up to turn it off, letting the first rays of morning sun filter into the cabin. It was chilly so she pulled a blanket up from the foot of the bed and drew it over them. Nick stirred and smiled in his sleep. She looked down at him tenderly, wanting to touch him, but afraid that he might wake. For a long time she sat gazing down at him, thinking about him, about her son and of the future.

At last she gave a little sigh, her decision made, and slipped from the bed to shower in the tiny bathroom and to dress, or at least to put on as many garments as she could find—one or two rather vital ones seemed to be unaccountably missing. Then she made a couple of mugs of coffee and carried one in to Nick, bending to kiss him awake.

He stirred and opened his eyes, putting a hand behind her head to pull her down and kiss her properly. "Why are you dressed? Come back to bed," he demanded imperiously.

She smiled "I'm a working girl, remember? I have to get back to Melmia to work on my story and phone my paper."

"Do that tomorrow."

He reached for her again, but Holly moved out of the way. "First things first, okay? Here, I've brought you some coffee."

With a reluctant groan, Nick sat up and looked at his watch. "It's barely seven o'clock."

"I know, but I want to tell them that I've got the story and to hold a space for it in next week's edition."

"All right, I'll drink this and take you straight back." He smiled and pulled her down onto his lap. "And while you're on to them, tell them that you won't be back for a few weeks, that you'll be taking a second honeymoon sailing around the Greek Islands."

He kissed her again, the coffee forgotten, until Holly laughingly reminded him.

She watched him as he dressed and shaved—remembering—so that it almost seemed as if time had stood still, that they had always been together like this. On the way back to Melmia he talked about which islands they would visit, steering the boat with one hand, the other around her waist, holding her close to him, enjoying the feel of her body against the length of his.

When they got to the harbor, he said, "Do what

you have to do quickly, darling, I'll be waiting here for you."

"What are you going to do?"

"I'll go and buy some stores in the town. Enough so that we can sail for a few days without having to put into port unless we want to." He grinned happily. "I've an idea we might just be too busy for any sight-seeing for quite a while."

He turned her around to kiss her goodbye and was surprised by the intensity with which she returned it and the way she clung to him. "Hey, what's this?" Nick put up a finger to her eyes as she blinked back sudden tears.

"I know, silly, isn't it?" Holly gazed at him for a long moment, as if she couldn't get her fill of looking at him, then she said quickly, urgently, "I love you, Nick," and clung to him again.

Putting his arms around her, he held her close. "I know, sweetheart. But we've got all the time in the world now."

Before he let her go he kissed her again and said, "Hurry back. I can't wait to get you to myself."

Holly smiled and walked quickly along to the *taverna*, turning at the top of the steps to look back and wave to him.

In her room, she quickly changed her clothes and then watched from the window and saw the fisherman from the boat she had hired come to the *taverna* for her. A few minutes later Nick left the *Argosy* and walked into the town. As soon as he was out of sight Holly picked up her suitcases and hurried down the stairs. The fisherman took her luggage while she paid her bill, and then she was running across the harbor to the boat, praying that Nick wouldn't come back unexpectedly and see her. She stood in the stern, watching anxiously as the boat got under way, but there was no sign of him and she slowly relaxed, gazing back at the island until it had become nothing more than a jagged outline against the horizon.

THE GREENNESS OF THE ENGLISH COUNTRYSIDE after the stark beauty of Greece was both welcome and overwhelming. The richness of trees and bushes, the deep green of lawns and undergrowth seemed to crowd in on the narrow lanes, trying to win them back. But it was good to be there, to smell the honeysuckle that grew against the cottage wall and to hold her son in her arms again. But there was time only for a few hours with him before she had to go to London, where Holly filed her story, receiving hearty congratulations from both the features editor and the editor himself. The photographs, too, were of a high standard, and they planned to make it the main feature for the following edition. Holly took advantage of the general air of approval and asked for a couple of weeks' holiday, which was given readily enough. But before going home to her cottage, Holly turned to her boss and said casually, "Oh, by the way, if a man called Falconer, Nick Falconer, should happen to ask for me, would you give him my home address, please."

"Okay, will do." He made a note on a pad. "What is he—a lead for another story?"

"Something like that," Holly agreed, turning to go home at last, and wondering bleakly whether he would ever be asked for the information.

It was three days before Nick came. Holly was up in the front bedroom of the cottage when she heard a car in the lane and looked out. It was a Saturday and Jamie was at home, playing in the garden in the sun, almost lost among the tall foxgloves and lupines as he looked for his new rabbit that he had let out of its cage yet again. The car pulled up outside, and Nick got out and walked up to the gate, checking the name on it to make sure he was at the right place. Holly drew back, suddenly breathless, her pulse racing.

As Nick lifted the latch Jamie heard it and emerged from the flowers, leaves in his hair and a smudge of dirt on his face. "Hello. I've lost my rabbit."

Nick grinned. "I'd better shut the gate, then." He crouched down to Jamie's level. "What color is it?"

"It's white and he hasn't got a name yet. Just Mr. Rabbit."

"Well, perhaps it's still in your own garden. Did you come through the hedge?"

Jamie frowned. "This *is* my garden. Mr. Rabbit lives in that cage over there that mommy made for me."

A puzzled look came into Nick's eyes as he sought to work out the situation. "Why didn't your daddy make it for you?"

Jamie's eyes, blue and innocent, looked up into Nick's face as he said simply, "I never had a daddy. He went away before I was borned. But mommy says I can look after her when I'm big enough instead," he added importantly.

Nick stood up suddenly and stared down at the

boy. In the window Holly raised her hand to her mouth, biting her knuckles hard, in an agony about what he would do next.

His face white, Nick said harshly, "What's your name?"

Jamie looked up at him uneasily, scared by his tone, and realized that this tall man was a stranger, and he'd been told never to talk to strangers. But despite his fear he faced up to him. "James Nicholas Falconer Weston," he answered in a breathless rush, because he'd only just learned it all and it was hard to remember.

Holly's heart lurched as she saw the look on Nick's face, saw him stare at his son and see his own features mirrored there. Slowly he went down onto his knees and put out a tentative hand to touch the child's hair, his mouth twisted almost in pain. Then he said hoarsely, "Hello, son," and pulled the boy to him to hold him very, very close.

Some instinct must have told Jamie that he was safe because he didn't cry or call out, but after a while he began to wriggle and Nick loosened his hold. He picked him up and stood up. "Let's go and find your mother, shall we?"

And suddenly life came back into her limbs, and Holly was flying down the stairs and through the hall. They were halfway up the path when she tumbled through the door and then stopped precipitately, her hair flying around her head.

Nick saw her and for a moment his eyes blazed with anger. "You idiot! You crazy, crazy idiot!" But then he held out his free arm to her and she ran to him, tears of happiness running down her cheeks.

Nick's eyes, too, were wet as he buried his head in her neck and said roughly, "Why the hell didn't you tell me?"

But it was some time later, when they had both recovered a little, and Jamie had gone off to look for his rabbit again, that Holly answered that question. She led him to the wooden seat under the old apple tree and said rather incoherently, "I didn't want you to come back to me because you *had* to. I wanted you to want to. I had to be sure, you see. Sure that it wasn't just a...a sexual hang-up. I thought that, perhaps, once we'd made love again you might realize that it *was* only sex you wanted after all, and you'd be glad I'd gone away. And I couldn't risk telling you about Jamie in case it made you think it was your duty to come back...or something stupid like that. You do see, don't you? I had to be sure that you loved me enough to come after me again."

"Oh, Holly." He put a hand on either side of her head and looked at her face for a long moment before he bent to kiss her hard on the mouth, his lips bruising in their need and intensity.

Too choked by emotion to speak, Holly buried her head in his shoulder when at last he let her go, and felt him stroke her hair.

"God, if I'd only known," Nick said thickly. "What you must have gone through to keep him and bring him up on your own. Didn't your parents help you at all?"

Holly straightened up and pushed the hair off her face with a trembling hand. "No, they wanted me to have an abortion and to divorce you. And ...and I couldn't do that, so I left. They . . . ." She bit her lip hard. "I suppose they must have destroyed your letter, and I must have left just before you came to look for me. I didn't think you wanted me anymore, you see." Her eyes looked up at him, dark and haunted. "Oh, Nick, if only I'd waited."

He swore savagely under his breath, then said urgently, "I'll make it up to you, my darling, I swear it." His hands gripped hers tightly, warm and strong. "I've been offered a directorship of my company, based here in London. We can be together always, the three of us."

"Oh, Nick." Holly moved into the safe haven of his arms, her happiness complete and overflowing as Nick kissed her again and again, as if he still couldn't believe that she was really his at last.

"Mommy, I found my rabbit." Jamie's piping voice interrupted them as he ran around the corner of the house, clutching the poor animal to him. "Why are you kissing that man?" he demanded suspiciously.

Nick laughed. "There was definitely a possessive note in that question. When are you going to tell him who I am, and that he'd better get used to seeing me kiss you?"

Holly stood up and held out her hand to him, her face radiant with love and happiness. "What's wrong with right now—and let's tell him together, shall we? Oh, Nick, we've both been waiting so long for you to come home!"

Take these
4 best-selling novels
FREE

That's right! FOUR first-rate Harlequin romance novels by four world renowned authors, FREE, as your introduction to the Harlequin Presents Subscription Plan. Be swept along by these FOUR exciting, poignant and sophisticated novels . . . . Travel to the Mediterranean island of Cyprus in **Anne Hampson**'s "Gates of Steel" . . . to Portugal for **Anne Mather**'s "Sweet Revenge" . . . to France and **Violet Winspear**'s "Devil in a Silver Room" . . . and the sprawling state of Texas for **Janet Dailey**'s "No Quarter Asked."

Harlequin Presents...

The very finest in romantic fiction

Join the millions of avid Harlequin readers all over the world who delight in the magic of a really exciting novel. SIX great NEW titles published EACH MONTH! Each month you will get to know exciting, interesting, true-to-life people . . . . You'll be swept to distant lands you've dreamed of visiting . . . . Intrigue, adventure, romance, and the destiny of many lives will thrill you through each Harlequin Presents novel.

Get all the latest books before they're sold out!
As a Harlequin subscriber you actually receive your personal copies of the latest Presents novels immediately after they come off the press, so you're sure of getting all 6 each month.

Cancel your subscription whenever you wish!
You don't have to buy any minimum number of books. Whenever you decide to stop your subscription just let us know and we'll cancel all further shipments.